'You could ma

Maggie felt her kne
she would have dropped to the floor if Phil
hadn't grabbed her.

'Think about it. We're already living together,
so the logistics would be simple. We work
together, so we understand the stresses of
each other's job—none better. The baby will
have a hands-on father, and we were great
together in bed.'

Maggie felt the air around her grow suddenly
colder, then heard Phil repeat the words in a
slow, hoarse voice.

'We were great together in bed!'

He stared at Maggie, disbelief and anger
vying for control of his features.

Anger won.

'Is it my baby, Maggie?' he asked, his voice
soft but no less furious for its softness. 'It is,
isn't it? And just when were you going to
share this little gem of knowledge with me?
Just how long did you intend letting me
believe it was someone else's?'

JIMMIE'S CHILDREN'S UNIT

*The Children's Cardiac Unit,
St James's Hospital, Sydney. A specialist unit
where the dedicated staff mend children's hearts...
and their own!*

The trilogy continues with
THE HEART SURGEON'S PROPOSAL.
Passion leads to pregnancy for anaesthetist Maggie,
and a practical proposal from surgeon Phil.
But Maggie won't accept a loveless marriage,
and Phil finds himself having to persuade her...

Don't miss the next story from Jimmie's—
THE ITALIAN SURGEON—
coming from Meredith Webber and Mills and Boon®
Medical Romance™ in September!

**JIMMIE'S CHILDREN'S UNIT
...where hearts are mended!**

THE HEART SURGEON'S PROPOSAL

BY
MEREDITH WEBBER

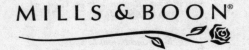

MILLS & BOON®

First published in Great Britain 2005
Harlequin Mills & Boon Limited,
Eton House, 18-24 Paradise Road, Richmond, Surrey TW9 1SR

© Meredith Webber 2005

ISBN 0 263 84312 2

Set in Times Roman 10½ on 12 pt.
03-0605-46775

Printed and bound in Spain
by Litografía Rosés, S.A., Barcelona

CHAPTER ONE

PHILIP PARK, paediatric surgical fellow of some standing and reputation, folded himself into the seat in the small, dingy space behind the pilot. The stuffiness in his head told him he'd spent far too long breathing recycled cigarette smoke in a club the previous evening, having refused to leave before a certain mini-skirted colleague had departed. And gritty eyes reminded him of the mostly sleepless night he'd spent wondering why this same colleague had accepted a lift home with one of those big bronzed Aussies that seemed to hang around all the beaches, and not with neat, clean, though fairly white-skinned, very English Phil!

So now he felt gnarly and out of sorts and totally irritated at being called out at the crack of dawn on a Sunday morning.

Added to which, he hated flying, hated small planes, hated retrievals—in fact, right now, he couldn't think of anything much he didn't hate.

He didn't hate his job. In fact, his job excited him more than any woman ever had.

Didn't really hate retrievals...

'You all saddled up back there?' the pilot asked. He was one of a group that called themselves, unbelievably, the Flying Marvels. They offered the planes and services as pilots, free of charge, to fly sick children from country areas to the city for treatment. They also donated their planes, time and piloting skills when organs became available for transplants and no government plane was available.

But in spite of the man's worthiness, Phil found himself scowling at the back of the man's head. Top of his hate list were cheery pilots! This one would probably say 'Up, up and away' as he took off.

'Up, up and away,' the pilot said minutes later, and Phil had to laugh, amusement easing his grumpiness, though not the tension knotting his stomach—tension in part due to the flight but also, he knew, building up because of what lay ahead.

Think of something else, he told himself, and almost as if he'd snapped a switch an image of a petite brunette slipped onto a screen in his mind.

Maggie Walsh!

Because thinking about Maggie was infinitely preferable to thinking about sudden death if this flying sardine can plummeted to earth, or thinking about the task awaiting him if they survived the journey, he trawled through his mind for the moment when taking Maggie Walsh to bed had seemed like an excellent idea.

He'd taken little enough notice of her—as a woman, not a doctor—six months ago when she'd been appointed as the anaesthetist on their team. She was a calm, quiet, very professional anaesthetist, so focussed on her work that although his male mind had registered the additional words 'attractive brunette', he had ignored them.

Then, a couple of times, when the surgical team had spent social time together, he'd seen another side of Maggie. Freed of the restraints of Theatre—and of 'hospital' clothes—she'd metamorphosed into a sexy, boot-wearing party girl. Not a drinker, or outrageous in her social behaviour, just a woman who enjoyed going out and dancing the night away.

In truth, the change had kind of spooked him and he'd found himself studying her more closely in Theatre and around the hospital, wondering which was the real Maggie Walsh.

That had been OK. It hadn't affected his work or anything, and he didn't think Maggie had known he was puzzled—attracted?—by her other self.

Until two nights ago, when something had happened between them—something so totally unexpected he was still finding it hard to believe. It hadn't been entirely his fault because late that night, in the privacy of her bedroom, Maggie's hands had been as desperate in stripping his clothes off as his had been stripping hers!

But it was the aftermath of that encounter—could mind-blowing sex be described baldly as an *encounter*?—that needed consideration.

Firstly, there was the weird feeling he'd had when he'd woken in the night to find Maggie's small but curvy body tucked up against his. Protective: that was how he'd felt, the sensation so alien to his usual feelings and moods he'd searched his mind for another description.

But, no, *protective* stuck.

Then, maybe because of the protective sensation, he'd reacted badly, retreating from further intimacy with her by flirting outrageously with Annie the following night—last night.

Not that Maggie had seemed to mind, giving him the impression that what had happened between them had meant nothing to her either.

Another image of Maggie flashed into his mind. Not the quiet, efficient anaesthetist he saw every day in

Theatre, but a pocket-siren in a red miniskirt, black lacy top and shiny red boots!

Maggie dressed to go out last night...

He must have groaned for both Kurt and the Flying Marvel turned.

'You OK?' the Flying Marvel asked. 'Sick bag in the pocket on the back of my seat.'

Phil glared at the pilot then reminded himself they were in his hands, so he couldn't wish any bad luck on the man. Seeking diversion from his Maggie thoughts, he looked at Kurt, sitting beside the pilot, his attention now refocussed on the Western he was reading. The man was one of the best operators Phil had ever seen on a heart-lung bypass machine, but as a conversationalist—well, one might as well talk to one of the machines he operated.

But thinking of the heart-lung machine reminded him of why they were flying from Sydney to Brisbane—reminded him of work.

Enough avoidance tactics! Time to seriously consider what lay ahead.

Waiting for them up in Brisbane was a SIDS baby— an infant who had died from sudden infant death syndrome.

Phil's heart went out to the parents of this unknown infant, grieving for a beloved baby, yet still finding in their hearts the ultimate generosity to donate the baby's organs so other infants might have a chance to live full and useful lives.

He would be but one surgeon in Theatre tonight— he and Kurt working together to take the baby's heart for a little girl who would otherwise die. Then, with the precious organ packed in a slush of ice, they'd fly back with it to Sydney.

Think of the procedure, he told himself, and a picture of a small healthy infant heart came up in his mind. Mentally he rehearsed how he'd operate to remove it with the aortic arch intact, so he and Alex Attwood, his boss and team leader at the new cardiac surgery unit at St James's Hospital, could attach it to the vessels in Amy Carter's tiny chest.

'It's your heart, you do it!'

Back at Jimmie's in Sydney some hours later, Phil heard the words but at first didn't understand them. He'd only been in Theatre a matter of minutes, moving into the first assistant's position to help Alex as he carefully removed Amy's defective heart.

Now adrenalin surged through him.

'Me? Do it? Do the transplant?'

'Come on, man, we don't want her on bypass any longer than necessary!'

Alex's order was curt, as well it might have been, and Phil responded as much to the tone of voice as to the words. He changed places with Alex, moving in beside Rachel, the American theatre sister they'd brought, with Kurt, from the States, and his hands went through a routine he'd seen a dozen times but had never done as the lead surgeon in an operation.

'Sats are good,' Maggie said, and her presence and quiet voice gave him added confidence. This was just another op, only he, not Alex, was the lead.

His fingers working surely in the cooled body, he inserted tiny stitches, sewing Amy's arteries and veins into place in the new heart. Each stitch had to be spaced with care, so the pressure of blood being pumped through her body wouldn't force them apart. Kurt counted off the time since Amy's heart had been removed and Maggie's regular reports reminded him how long she'd been unconscious, and how her body was standing up to the bypass machine. Blood values told them Amy was OK, but the real test would come after the operation.

Then the new heart was stimulated with drugs and the silence in Theatre became absolute as they all waited to see if it would beat—and if the carefully stitched veins and arteries would hold.

'Yay!'

The cheer went up from Rachel, the first to see the rhythmic movement of the heart muscles as they squeezed blood from the atria to the ventricles and out into the arteries.

'Well done,' Alex said quietly, and Phil felt his knees turn to jelly with relief, though as he'd worked he hadn't been aware of the terrible tension building up in his body. He glanced involuntarily towards Maggie. Hoping for her praise as well?

Whatever!

It didn't happen. She was watching the screen of the monitor, oblivious to his presence—or his need for reassurance.

Forget Maggie and concentrate on Amy!

'Should I close her chest or use a patch?' he asked Alex, knowing there was a likelihood of the new heart swelling in protest to the trauma it had undergone.

'She's got such a small thoracic cavity I'd use the patch,' Alex said, and Rachel nodded to the circulating nurse to pass over one of the sealed envelopes, each holding a fine silicone rubber patch.

Across from him, Alex was explaining to Scott Douglas, the surgical registrar assisting, that the patch would keep the wound sterile while maximising the space inside Amy's chest.

'In a couple of days,' Alex added, as Phil sewed the thin filmy material meticulously into place, 'we'll operate again to remove the patch and close Amy's chest.'

Inserting the final stitch, overseeing the taping of the drains and tubes and wires attached to Amy's tiny body—it all took time, but finally they were done.

'I'll take her into the PICU,' Maggie said, and Phil, who was feeling so elated to have successfully completed the op, wondered how she could possibly be so calm.

'Because I have to be,' she told him later, when, with an intensivist watching their charge, he persuaded her to go down to the canteen for lunch—a colleague-with-colleague lunch. 'I know you and Alex are exceptional surgeons, but even with you two there, things can go wrong, and while everyone else is cursing and swearing—and don't bother telling me you don't—someone has to remain calm.'

Her lips teased into a smile, and he remembered how that same teasing smile had set him on fire as they'd danced at the club.

It still set him on fire, although a hospital corridor was a most inappropriate place to be feeling lusty heat for a colleague. Not that he intended acting on it. He avoided relationships with close colleagues—too much fall-out when things ended!

He put his arm behind her back to guide her into the lift and looked at her, a small, pretty woman, with dark hair and even darker eyes, velvety dark—night sky in a hospital lift...

'First transplant I've been part of so the first time

I've seen a skin patch used on a baby. Do you always use one in transplants?'

As he usually had a post-op high himself, he understood why she'd be thinking about Amy, but he still felt a twinge of disappointment that the matter in the forefront of his mind right now—the night they'd spent together—had no place at all in hers.

He shook his head, hoping to clear it of wayward thoughts, and the velvet brown eyes looked puzzled.

'You don't know? But you worked so surely, and confidently, and calmly, and competently in there, I thought you must have done plenty of transplants. I was terrified—shaking like a leaf—although I kept telling myself it was just another op. It seems so—so omnipotent somehow!'

Phil smiled at her choice of words.

'Don't go saying things like that to Alexander the Great,' he teased. 'He's already given god-like status by most of his patients' parents.'

He paused, gathering his thoughts, telling himself it was good to be with Maggie, even if they were only talking work.

'It's not omnipotence, just good surgical work. If you think of the advances in medicine in the last century—especially in your field—you realise it's the researchers who should get all the praise. The people who made anaesthesia safer, or who went before us in surgical fields, developing techniques, working out how to keep a patient alive on a bypass machine—these are the ones who need the praise. We're just good technicians, following paths others forged for us.'

The lift had stopped, but before stepping out Maggie smiled at him.

'Super-duper technicians,' she said, and Phil felt a little hitch in the region of his heart.

It must be post-op excitement kicking in.

Couldn't possibly be to do with Maggie's smile.

He didn't do heart hitches where women were concerned.

CHAPTER TWO

Six weeks later

'So, YOU see, Min, given what happened between Maggie and me that one night, it's going to be awkward to say the least with her living here.'

So much had happened in the interim. Amy, the little girl on whom Phil had done the transplant, had thrown up every complication known to man, and some not known ones as well; then Annie, their unit manager, had been shot, leading to the revelation that Alex, his boss and landlord, was madly in love with her, and the two were getting married. With the drama and wedding preparations on top of their usual heavy workload, there'd been no time for socialising for any members of the team.

'It's been chaotic, Min.'

He scratched the tummy of the little bundle of black curls nestled on his lap and smiled at the sympathetic glance the soft brown eyes of Alex's dog cast his way. Though maybe the look was a 'keep scratching' look, not one of sympathy, as Minnie was now pushing one paw against his hand in a 'don't stop now' kind of way.

'I have to stop,' Phil told her, setting her back down on the floor. 'That was a car pulling up out the back and I've got to do the right thing and welcome Maggie to her new home. Carry suitcases, act the part of the genial host.'

Phil stood up, straightened his shoulders and rehearsed his best welcoming smile. Even without a mirror in the room, he knew it was a poor effort. He'd never felt less welcoming.

'This is ridiculous,' he muttered as he made his way through the house towards the back door. 'I'm thirty-four years old, a surgical fellow to one of the best paediatric heart surgeons in the world, a noted wooer and winner of women, housebroken to the extent I can clean and cook, well off, a good catch, as they say, and a little snip of an anaesthetist has got me flummoxed.'

Minnie, capering gaily around his feet, probably didn't understand the word 'flummoxed', and she certainly didn't understand that while they were intending to be politely welcoming, they weren't going to exhibit any signs of hysterical delight over Maggie moving in.

The moment Phil opened the door she was racing across the back yard to leap and cavort around Maggie's feet—literally dancing with excitement at the arrival of the new housemate.

'I'll get the rest,' Phil offered, as Maggie, with a backpack slung across one shoulder, towed a medium-sized red suitcase along the path to the back door.

'There is no rest,' she said.

'No rest? You've fitted *all* your clothes and four pairs of boots into that case? And don't tell me you don't have four pairs of boots, I've seen you in at least that many. The black ones you wore to the wedding yesterday, a brown pair you had on one weekend when I saw you at the hospital, another pair that look like snakeskin you were wearing when you went out with that juvenile intensivist in Melbourne, and the red ones you wore to the nightclub with Annie!'

Maggie stopped wheeling and laughed, little lines crinkling the corners of her usually serious dark eyes.

'Philip Park! Do you have a shoe fetish that you remember all my boots?' She shifted her attention from him to the dog. 'Oh, dear, Minnie, what have I got myself into here?'

See! Phil wanted to say to the same dog. See what I have to put up with from her! But Minnie had obviously gone all female and would undoubtedly side with Maggie.

'Actually, I shifted the rest of my stuff in before Alex and Annie's wedding,' Maggie continued, moving again, the suitcase *and* the dog now following her. 'Alex cleared all his things out of his room so I could start unpacking. Last weekend. Alex insisted you take time off and you flew up to the Gold Coast with Becky, didn't you?'

'I flew up to the Gold Coast, but not, if you must know, with Becky,' Phil muttered, wondering why things this woman said pushed his buttons when someone else saying them wouldn't affect him at all.

'Some other blonde, then?' Maggie said blithely, reaching the kitchen and snapping the towing handle of her case back into place, then bending to lift it.

Fuming over the 'blonde' dig, but not forgetful of his manners, Phil reached to take it from her and nearly knocked her over, recovering quickly enough to grab her arm to steady her.

'Sorry! Don't usually send new housemates flying as a way of introduction.'

And don't touch her again, he added to himself, as the awareness he was trying to keep at bay flared through his body.

Maggie looked into his blue eyes, wondering where the smile that usually lurked there had gone.

Just as well it had. Living with Phil was going to be

bad enough, but it would be infinitely harder if he'd kept smiling and twinkling those devastating eyes in her direction.

Why on earth had she agreed to this crazy scheme?

So the newlyweds Alex and Annie could have some privacy at Annie's place—that was why, she reminded herself.

'I'll carry this upstairs for you,' Phil said, and Maggie stepped back, determined not to have any more physical contact between them, no matter how accidental it might be.

'Thanks.'

She followed him up the stairs, her eyes taking note of the set of his shoulders, of the lithe way he moved, her body remembering other movements, her head repeating a sharp refrain—*madness, madness, madness*—because that's what moving in with Phil was. Total and utter madness!

Especially now.

Especially with what was in the case he carried, though she knew taking a second pregnancy test was useless. It would show exactly what the first one had—that she was carrying Phil's baby.

Some of the cocktail of fear, despair, excitement, trepidation and confusion inside her must have escaped in an involuntary cry, for Phil reached the top of the stairs and turned.

'You OK?'

'Fine, just fine,' she said, and indeed she was.

Physically fine.

Mentally she was almost deranged with thinking about it. About being pregnant!

Again!

Would it be all right this time?

She tamped down the now-familiar flutter of fear, and told herself fretting over how it had happened when Phil had used protection was pointless.

It *had* happened but, given her previous miscarriages—back when she'd been married to Jack—was she likely to keep it? Have a live baby?

And if she did, could she juggle work and a baby?

Time enough to decide what to do—and how to tell Phil—when she'd carried it safely for three months.

Tell Phil? Hell and damnation—how *had* it happened?

'There. Is there anything else you need brought up? Do you want time to unpack? We should sit down and talk about household things some time, I suppose. What you like to eat, cooking rosters, shopping, all that stuff. Alex and I did what suited us—if there was no food in the house and I was here, I shopped. It worked most of the time, but you might like something more structured. Mrs Hobbs, the cleaning lady, comes on Thursdays, and she puts on loads of washing and comes back Friday mornings to iron.'

Phil was looking over Maggie's shoulder, out through the front window, as he imparted this information and Maggie realised he probably felt as awkward about the night they'd spent together as she did.

Well, not quite as awkward, given the baby, but perhaps she should clear the air.

She took a deep breath and started right in.

'Look, Phil, with Annie being shot, Alex going out of his mind with worry and the resulting pressure of extra work at the hospital, we haven't had much chance to talk to each other about that night. But we can't go on pretending what happened didn't happen. It did, and I enjoyed it and have no regrets—' well, maybe one which he didn't need to know about—yet! '—but we're going to be living together and we need to move on.'

'That's it?' he said. 'We need to *move on*? That's all it meant to you?' He was practically yelling the words at her.

Oh, dear! Now she'd hurt his ego, or whatever part of a man's mental make-up was attached to his sexual prowess. But she could hardly tell him that it had been like all her dreams coming true, that she'd been attracted to him from the first time they'd met six months ago—not when he had no idea how she felt about him and when he certainly wasn't even part way to falling in love with her.

Not when he usually took no more notice of her than he did of the furniture in their suite of rooms at work.

'Phil, we went out to dinner in a group, went on from there to a club and danced, got worked up and, being consenting adults, fell lustily into bed together. What was it meant to mean?'

Huge frown from Phil.

'Something more than it did to you, obviously,' he growled, adding under his breath, 'Fell lustily into bed! Move on!'

'But you can't make it more than it was,' she protested. 'It wasn't as if you'd been chasing me around the hospital corridors since we first met, or that we'd been dating and it was the next step in a relationship. It happened, that's all.'

'That's all!' he muttered, echoing her words but not the placating way she'd said them. Then he stalked out of her bedroom and clumped down the stairs, apparently meeting Minnie on the way for she heard him grumbling away to someone.

Realising her legs had become a little shaky, Maggie made her way to the bed and sank down on it.

Had she made a mistake, bringing up the subject at all? Or was it her minimising it—surely the only option, considering they'd be living together—that had upset Phil?

No answer to either question sprang to mind, so she stood up and crossed to her suitcase, unpacking it, putting clothes away, finding the new packet from the chemist and setting it down in the *en suite* bathroom. Then, because she wanted to leave it another week before she did a second test, and remembering the cleaning lady, she put it in the cupboard under the basin.

Another deep breath and it was time to go downstairs and join him. Time to discuss shopping and cooking, and pretend this was a normal house-sharing arrangement between two colleagues.

Yeah, right!

Phil heard the floor creak as she moved about upstairs, and reminded himself that at least she wasn't wearing boots. His libido was already running amok where Maggie was concerned, but had she been wearing the red numbers, he'd find it even harder to restrain himself from ravishing her right here on the kitchen table.

Though why he still wanted to, he had no idea.

Cool as a cucumber, she'd brushed him off. About the only thing she hadn't said to destroy his self-confidence had been that the sex had been forgettable. Although 'enjoyed it' was hardly high praise.

Probably next to forgettable, come to think about it.

'Pathetic, that's what it is, Minnie,' he complained to the dog who, missing Alex, had once again found her way onto his lap. 'It's not as if my self-worth and self-confidence are tied to my sexual prowess!'

Footsteps on the stairs—get a grip! They were house-sharing colleagues.

She breezed in and bent to pat Minnie, who'd leapt off his knee to greet her then settled at the other side of the table, though not far enough away for him to avoid the faint hint of perfume that seemed the only thing common to the two Maggies.

'Lilacs!' he said, and knew from her questioning glance she had no idea what he was talking about.

'The perfume you wear. I've been wondering for months what it reminded me of and it just struck me. Lilacs flowering in the garden at home. You notice the perfume most at night when it seems to scent the air all over the property.'

'Do you miss home?'

The question startled him, but not nearly as much as the look of genuine interest and concern on Maggie's face.

If she but knew!

'Not really,' he said, then something prompted him to add, 'I'm not quite sure where home is—in a permanent sense.'

'But home is where you grew up, surely!' A puzzled frown accompanied the words. 'I haven't lived at home for years, not in the house where I grew up, but it will always be home to me. Though I guess home is more a concept—a "whole-of-family" kind of thing.'

'Yes, well, family's nearly as alien to me as home.' Phil stood up and moved to fill the kettle, hoping his curt tone and his movement would be enough to signal the conversation was at an end.

'Alien? In what way?'

Persistence in a small package!

He could ignore her, but he had a feeling she'd just keep asking, so he sighed, rested his hands on the sink and looked out the kitchen window as he replied.

'I'm not sure about the concept of home, Mags, because I grew up in a house. It might have had beautiful gardens and lilacs that bloomed in spring, nannies, servants, horses, dogs and cats, but it was a house, not a home. I had a brother, a sister, a mother and a father— I have all but the father still, though his death made little difference, he was never there—and even now, when my mother writes dutifully once a week, she says things like, ''Your brother has a new car, your grandfather kicked the cat.'' No one has a name and surely in homes, people have names.'

'Mags! I like that,' Maggie managed to say, though her chest was filled to overflowing with pity for the man who stood, turned away from her, shoulders bent as he revealed the poverty of his wealthy upbringing. She longed to go to him—to press her body against his back and put her arms around his waist, holding him in silent empathy. But something told her Phil hadn't shared this information with many people, and was probably already regretting having told her.

She'd have to be very careful how she treated it.

And him.

Especially him. No way could she let pity intrude into her determination to keep him at arm's length. Her body might shimmy with delight at even the most casual of touches, but embarking on a physical relationship with Phil would make things even more complex than they already were.

Especially when it would mean nothing more to him than physical pleasure…

'Coffee?'

Maggie breathed easily again, aware they'd negotiated a very delicate situation and got things back to normal.

'Black, two sugars,' she said, thinking about her relief, not the content of what she'd said, so she was surprised when he spun towards her.

'Two sugars? You? I know you're always drinking coffee so, with all the sugar, why don't you put on weight?'

His eyes were scanning her body to see where sixteen teaspoons of sugar per day might be showing themselves in unsightly bulges.

'I dance it off,' she told him. 'That's why I'm crazy about going out to clubs where there's dancing. I tried a gym membership at one time, and did one session. It was the most boring, tedious hour of my life and, believe me, as an anaesthetist I know about boring and tedious. From then on I stuck with dancing.'

Phil wished with all his heart she hadn't said that, because it brought back the night they'd danced and danced together, the music and the contact, and though a lot of it had been little more than occasional touches, it had primed them both for love.

He remembered how she'd felt in his arms—small, and warm, and cuddly in the final, slower dance—and his body, which had been on full alert since Maggie had entered the house, now went into demand mode.

He concentrated on making coffee, stirred the two spoons of sugar—heaped, so she'd need to dance again—into it, then brought both cups over to the table.

'We'll put sugar on the shopping list,' he joked, and wasn't at all surprised to hear his voice come out exceedingly croaky.

'Do we need a shopping list? Should we shop today?'

Once again, Phil felt relief. So far things weren't going too badly. Maggie seemed to have the ability to sail right over the awkward bits, which meant she was either totally insensitive or very adept at putting her fellow man at ease.

Whichever it was, long may it continue while he was the fellow man in question!

'We should. What with Alex spending most of the last month down at Annie's place, then the wedding preparations, we've done very little shopping and the pantry's almost bare.'

Maggie got up and crossed to it, familiar with the layout of the kitchen as she'd been living four doors down in Annie's house, which had a similar floor plan.

'You're right,' she told him, 'though Minnie either eats an inordinate amount for such a small dog, or every time either of you shopped you bought food for her.'

Minnie, hearing her name, got up from beneath the table and trotted across to look hopefully up at Maggie.

'Don't try that soft brown begging eyes stuff on me,' Maggie said sternly. 'I bet you have regular mealtimes and a proper amount of food at each. You go begging for food and you'll get as fat as a fool because you can't dance it off.'

The conversation eased a lot of Phil's tension and by the time he'd explained Minnie's routine and they'd made out a shopping list, he could almost believe this 'nothing-more-than-colleagues-sharing-a-house' pretence he'd engaged in might work.

'I love cooking, so I'm happy to cook if I'm home,' Maggie offered, and Phil smiled at her.

'Which means I get to stack the dishwasher—I'm good at that.'

'And unstack it,' she reminded him. 'That's part and parcel of the dishwasher job!'

They were arguing amiably about how to stack dishwashers and whether they'd shop before or after lunch when first his and then Maggie's pager buzzed.

'Hospital,' he said, getting up and moving to phone in.

'I'll change my shoes and be right down,' Maggie told him. 'You can fill me in on what's happening as we walk up the road.'

She will *not* be changing into boots, Phil told himself as he rinsed the coffee cups and stacked them on the top shelf—his choice of placement, not Maggie's—of the dishwasher.

CHAPTER THREE

'It's a newborn—male—with aortic stenosis,' Phil began as they walked the short distance to the hospital.

'Narrowing or failure of the aortic valve showing as congestive heart failure and shock?' Maggie queried, thinking of the symptoms and trying not to think of the wee infant suffering them, or his desperately anxious parents. 'Did they have pre-warning something was wrong, and what are they doing for him now?'

'Apparently they had no pre-warning. No recent scans to show something might be amiss. The baby was born in a small birthing unit in an outer suburb, and the midwife heard a heart murmur and had the mother and child transferred straight to Jimmie's. The paediatrician called in a cardiologist, who's done scans which show the valve problem. He tried a balloon valvuloplasty to open the valves, but it didn't work.'

'There are probably associated problems,' Maggie muttered, shaking her head of the enormity of what the little baby was going through. 'Don't you usually find ventricular dysfunction—often left ventricle insufficiency—in these cases?'

'Yes, and the real problem is that surgery to correct aortic valves—'

He stopped, and Maggie, sensing something big lay beyond the beginning of the sentence, didn't press for more while he was thinking things through, but she wondered just what he hadn't said.

She found out a little later, as he argued with the cardiologist.

'I know from what you tell me the case is urgent, but every study done on AS in neonates shows a far greater chance of success with open surgery for valve repair in infants over one month. Even catheterisation repairs are more effective and last longer if the infant is a little older.'

'I've told the parents you can operate,' the cardiologist, someone Maggie hadn't met before, told Phil.

'Before I saw the child? You had no right to do that!'

'No? Seems to me it was the right thing to do, the way you're acting. I don't want you near the child at all if all you're going to do is cause problems.'

Maggie could sense Phil stiffening, and hear his determination to do the right thing in the way his voice became far more 'English', but he was still trying to placate the specialist.

'Look, we can use supportive management on the little chap until he's older. Prostaglandin to keep the ductus arteriosis open. The right ventricle in a neonate can keep blood flowing adequately through the whole body and newborns can tolerate less oxygen in their blood.'

'I have problems with prolonged use of prostaglandin,' the cardiologist said in a pompous voice bound to rile his listeners, 'but if you don't feel capable of doing the operation, then I suppose we'll have to try it. At least until your boss returns.'

He certainly riled Maggie.

'Excuse me!' she burst out, able to stand the man's snooty attitude no longer. 'I've been in Theatre when both Dr Attwood and Dr Park have been operating, and if you just watch their hands you could not tell which is which. Both are excellent surgeons with the figures from their successes to back this up. If Dr Park thinks this baby is too young for the surgery you want to inflict on him, he'll have solid statistics to prove it. You want to give him some figures, Phil?'

Phil smiled at her, but once again there was no smile lurking in his eyes, and she guessed the man's slur about waiting for Alex had bitten deep.

'I don't think there's any need for that. There are other paediatric cardiac surgeons in town. Dr Ellis might want to consult one of them.'

'I will!' The angry cardiologist spat the words at them, and strode away.

'Should we see the baby? The parents?' Maggie asked, watching Phil watch the man disappear, and wanting desperately to wipe the look of anguish from his face.

'We can't just barge in. The little chap's not our patient,' Phil reminded her. 'Ellis made that perfectly clear.'

'Yet you're desperately worried about him,' Maggie said, reading the expression on his face with ease.

'Because I know Dave Edwards, Alex's mate at Children's, is out of town for the weekend, and he's the only other surgeon I know here who'd be capable of doing the operation if the decision is made to go ahead.'

The full import of this struck home, and unconsciously Maggie's hand strayed to her own belly, where an embryo the size of a bean was currently producing its first organ—a heart!

'You think someone who might not have done one before—someone with less skill than you—will do it?'

'If Ellis can talk them into it!'

He rubbed his hands across his face and threaded his fingers through his hair, a gesture she'd never seen before but so redolent of despair her heart ached for him.

'Hell, Maggie, what do I decide? Is it the parents' choice? The cardiologist's? Or mine? I'd choose to not do it right now and I could explain that to the parents, tell them why it's better to wait, but I can't talk to them because that baby isn't my patient. Yet if Ellis persuades someone else to do it and the baby dies, will I, in part, be responsible?'

Maggie put her arm around his waist and hugged him close to her side. Bother the physical consequences. If ever a man needed a hug it was this man, and he needed it now.

'You and Alex make life-and-death decisions all the time,' she reminded him. 'You've held the lives of so many babies in your hands, but you know you can't save them all. Can you pretend this baby is in Melbourne, or somewhere else where it's physically impossible for you to be involved? Would that help?'

He smiled down at her and touched his finger to her cheek.

'Not much, but you do, though I have a feeling this could get nasty and you should distance yourself from the whole affair so you don't get hit by any of the fall-out.'

'Nasty?' Maggie queried, battling the urge to press her hand against the place where his finger had touched her cheek. 'Fall-out?'

'Annie's away as well, remember—which means we don't have a unit manager to fight our in-hospital battles. Ellis is powerful in this hospital and we're the relative new chums.'

'The hospital could make you do the op? But it

can't—not if you feel it's not in the best interests of
the baby!'

Phil smiled again, but it was a weak effort.

'They can't make me operate, but they can make
things uncomfortable for the unit—and for Annie and
Alex when they return.'

'Damn hospital politics!' Maggie muttered. 'I can't
believe it can intrude into decisions like this. I'd like
to walk out right now, but I guess you don't want to.'

She'd put a little space between them but could still
feel the shape of Phil's body against hers.

She needed a diversion.

She needed a coffee!

'Seeing as we're here, let's have another cup of coffee. I barely drank half of the last one.'

She led the way towards their suite of rooms where
Annie had installed a state-of-the-art coffee-maker.

'Dr Park!'

Maggie recognised the voice of the hospital CEO,
Col Bennett, though how Dr Ellis had got him to the
hospital so quickly on a Sunday she couldn't guess.
She turned with Phil and stood beside him as Col, with
Dr Ellis yapping at his heels, approached.

'Dr Ellis tells me you don't feel confident about performing this operation.'

Maggie glared at the doctor mentioned, unable to
believe his effrontery and misrepresentation of the
facts. But if she was annoyed, it was nothing to the
anger sparking from Phil's body.

'I am not confident of a successful outcome in so
young a baby. It is my considered opinion that the operation should be delayed until the infant is older. I can
produce a whole body of evidence that the operations
to correct valvular aortic stenosis are more successful

on babies over thirty days. The figures on operating on a neonate are abysmal to say the least. And as we can, and have in the past, successfully kept neonates with this condition alive for thirty days, I see no reason why Dr Ellis can't accept this case management.'

'Oh!' Col said, but before he could say more, Dr Ellis broke in with a long dissertation on the damage prostaglandin could do and why supportive measures, in this case, wouldn't work.

He was positively bristling with anger.

'You haven't yet seen the infant,' he fired at Phil.

'Because he is not, as yet, my patient,' Phil fired right back. 'Come on, Maggie, let's get that coffee.'

He took her by the arm and hustled her away, muttering when they were far enough for his words not to be heard, 'I'd have hit that man if I'd stayed there a second longer!'

Maggie pressed her hand against his, which was still on her upper arm, steering her along the passageway.

'Far better to walk away than to come to blows in the unit, but I can't blame you for wanting to wipe the smug smirk off that fellow's face. I wanted to slap it myself.'

They walked into the suite and she turned on the coffee-machine then found ground coffee and filter papers and set everything in motion.

'What I don't understand,' she said to Phil, who'd walked to the desk he used and was booting up his computer, 'is why Ellis is so adamant about the operation. Don't cardiologists usually prefer to go the medication or closed catheterisation route in most cases?'

'They do,' Phil said, his voice vague as if most of his attention was on his computer screen. 'But apparently the catheterisation didn't work, so it's my guess there's so much wrong with that poor baby, Ellis is afraid he'll die, and, having been called in as the specialist, he doesn't want the death on his hands. He'd far rather the baby died on the operating table, or from post-op complications. That way it's not his fault.'

He paused then added, 'And there's a more than fifty per cent chance—up to sixty-eight per cent chance, in fact—of that happening if he's operated on this young. I just don't believe the risks are worth that kind of result when by waiting, even a short time, the odds are considerably reduced.'

Maggie carried his coffee across to him and perched on the other side of his desk. He looked up at her and grinned.

'Thanks for sticking by me,' he said, and her heart turned over in her chest. The grin, the words—the man's dogged determination to do the right thing—all combined to remind her that what she'd felt for Phil had grown from the initial attraction at that first meeting to something very close to love.

Oh, dear!

Better to think about work.

'Is Dr Ellis right about prolonged use of prostaglandin? Are there concerns?'

'Yes. Various studies have shown problems with prolonged use of it, but it's been done often enough for intensivists to know how to handle the side-effects. It's politics again. Ellis has voiced these concerns to Col because the baby could well die anyway, and once again he will have someone to blame—me, for suggesting the prostaglandin option!'

'You keep talking about blame but surely this is one very sick baby who, without any supportive measures, would probably be already dead. In fact, the parents

have probably already been offered the option of compassionate care—keeping the baby comfortable but not
intervening in his condition. There shouldn't be any
talk of blame. If the baby dies, it's no one's fault.'

Phil turned his attention from the computer screen
to smile at her and she had to remind herself it was
nothing but a colleague-to-colleague smile.

'Of course there shouldn't be blame laid at individual doors, but it happens every day. Everyone likes to
palm off responsibility—you see it everywhere. Surely
you've been in an op that's gone wrong—who's the
first person the surgeon blames?'

Maggie smiled back at him—colleague-to-
colleague!—although every smile from Phil caused an
achy feeling in her heart.

'The anaesthetist—or sometimes the theatre sister.
Sometimes even the assisting surgeon. You're right,
it's a fairly normal, if unattractive, human trait to look
around for somewhere to lay blame. But surely not in
the death of a baby born with so many complications
he might not survive anyway.'

'Wishful thinking, Mags!' Phil said, his attention
now back on the screen as his fingers clicked keys to
scroll through the information he'd brought up.

Mags again! No one had ever called her that. The
thought warmed little corners of her body.

Sweet heaven! Was she going soupy over a nick-
name?

She sipped her coffee, watching Phil scanning the
information on the screen, knowing he was so intent
on what he was doing she could study him for a while.

Brown hair, slightly lightened, maybe by his weekend in the sun, longish and very straight, dropping forward over his forehead, touching his ears. Darker eye-

brows—she could only see one, but knew the pair matched well—above the mid-blue eyes that caused flip-flops in her heart region when they smiled at her.

No smiling eyes recently, which, she told herself firmly, was a good thing. If her stomach was about to launch an early morning rebellion, she could do without heart flip-flops at the same time.

She continued her study, taking in the neat nose with a slight dip at the end—a Roman nose, she rather thought, although she'd never done much nose-typing. Clean-shaven pale skin, but she guessed from the shadow his beard was darker than his hair. Nice chin, not too obvious, with an indentation too slight to be a dimple but tempting her fingers to touch it every time she noticed it there.

You missed the lips, a snide voice in her head reminded her, and she turned away because just looking at those lips reminded her of kisses, and made her ache for more of them. But life was complicated enough already, without adding Phil's kisses to the mix.

'There it is—I knew I'd read it recently. Latest studies confirm that patients over thirty days fare far better short-term and have a higher long-term chance of survival than those operated on as neonates. I'll print this out and wave it in the face of the next person who mentions it.'

His fingers, long and thin, danced across the keyboard, and as the printer on the far side of the room began to chatter, the phone on Annie's desk rang and Maggie crossed to answer it.

'It's Alex, for you,' she said quietly, waving the receiver in his direction.

Phil cursed under his breath, but picked up the extension on his desk.

'Alex, I assume you're phoning about Dr Ellis's patient. Believe me, man, I'd as soon have operated as dragged you into this mess.'

'Don't give it a thought,' Alex responded. 'Col Bennett got me on my mobile and I told him exactly what you'd already told him. I just thought you might need some moral support.'

'Thanks, I appreciate it, and now you're on the phone, how do I actually stand within the hospital? I know they can't force me to perform an operation I truly believe will do more harm than good, but am I going to jeopardise your position or put pressure on the continuation of the unit? I know we're on fairly precarious ground as it is, with other services and units jealous of the money we've been allocated. Is this going to make things more difficult for you?'

'Too bad if it does, and as for your position, you're my fellow, employed and paid by me, so hang tough.'

They talked some more, Phil explaining what he knew about the patient, Alex confirming his own belief that the operation should be delayed as long as possible, running through the figures Phil had already considered, then repeating his opinion that Phil had done the right thing.

Phil knew he shouldn't feel relieved—he'd already had high cardiac surgical standing before joining Alex to learn more about the paediatric side of things—but he was.

'Thanks again,' he said. 'Now, you get back to looking after Annie and enjoying your honeymoon, while we hold the fort here.'

He hung up and picked up the now lukewarm cup of coffee. He sipped at it and grimaced, then smiled at Maggie who was perched on Annie's desk.

'Seems we're doomed as far as coffee is concerned today. Shall we give it up as a bad job, get the car and go shopping?'

She looked surprised but slipped off the desk and picked up her handbag.

'Sure. Why not?'

He knew she was humouring him, but couldn't explain his need to get out of the hospital. Maybe if he put his mind to something else he could forget about the ill baby. Forget that just maybe, by refusing to operate, he was denying the little fellow a slim chance of life.

'You're worrying about him, aren't you?' Maggie said a little later, removing the second, third and fourth bottles of coffee he'd absent-mindedly loaded into the trolley.

'Yes!'

'What did Alex say?'

'That I'd done the right thing—that he wouldn't operate either. We do some unavoidable procedures in neonates—do them all the time—but the heart muscle is so slushy in a newborn, doing anything is a risk. But that's not the issue, Mags. It's the voice in my head that's bothering me.'

'A voice suggesting an op at this stage might just save him?'

Phil smiled at his companion. She was wearing a red sweater and he wondered if maybe red was her favourite out-of-hospital colour. It was a cheery colour and he felt inexplicably cheered. By her presence and understanding more than the red sweater, but still...

'Damn voices!' he admitted and she laughed.

'We all have them. *Why didn't you try such and*

such? mine will ask when a protocol goes wrong, although I know full well it should have worked.'

And standing in the beverages aisle of the local supermarket, Phil was struck by how good it was to have Maggie around. As a colleague and a friend. He doubted he could remove lust from the equation altogether, but he could hide it, and enjoy her company both as a workmate and a housemate.

'You two taking up residence in front of the coffee?'

An impatient shopper reminded him of where they were, and he grabbed the trolley and began to steer it out of that aisle and into the next, pausing when Maggie stopped to select an item, pushing again as she moved on, telling himself this was the same as the occasional times he and Alex had shopped together and he shouldn't be feeling any more pleasure because it was Maggie sharing the task.

'OK, all done. We'll go to the greengrocer then home,' she said cheerfully, some half an hour later.

'There's that word again,' Phil said, because he *had* been feeling more pleasure shopping with Maggie.

She turned towards him, her brow crinkling with confusion so for a moment she looked like a puzzled child.

'Greengrocer?' she asked, and Phil had to laugh.

'Home,' he corrected, reaching out and ruffling her short dark hair.

Her dark eyes mirrored her concern as she said, 'Oh, Phil!' very softly, then turned her attention back to unloading the trolley onto the checkout counter.

'I'll pay for this—we're using your car and your fuel,' he said, feeling a need to take control after her murmuring of his name had loosened something inside him.

Anatomically, this was unlikely. He was a cardiac surgeon, he knew people didn't have heart-strings so it couldn't be those.

'You won't pay. We'll split it and later set up a housekeeping system so we both pay the same,' she told him, the practical anaesthetist Maggie back in place, although he could have sworn it was the other Maggie who had whispered his name.

But as she drove efficiently out of the shopping-centre car park, he realised they weren't done with the conversation.

'Do you have some mental image of the home you'd have liked to have?' she asked. 'Does the word conjure up mental pictures for you?'

He turned to look at her, wondering if she was just making conversation or really wanted to know. He couldn't think why she would, but from what he knew of Maggie, she didn't talk for the sake of it.

Anyway, she was his housemate and he liked her and so...

'If I tell you, you'll probably laugh!' he said.

She glanced his way, brow wrinkled again.

'Why would I laugh? I really want to know. I'm trying to put myself in your shoes—growing up as you did. I know when I was growing up, one of five kids, I longed to be an only child, with a bedroom of my own, and to live on a farm where I could keep a horse and ducks and geese. I never went much on chickens, but I had a thing for fluffy yellow ducklings.'

'Well, we had the horse and ducks and geese, though I remember ducks as creatures with no discretion at all when it came to where they did their business. Duck poo everywhere down by the lake.'

'I suppose there's a downside to everything,' Maggie

said, pulling into the lane that ran behind the row of houses and provided access to the garages. 'But I'm not going to be diverted by duck poo. Tell me about your dream.'

Phil sighed. He'd been right about her persistence.

'It's stupid,' he began, feeling narky at being forced to talk about something so trivial. Then suddenly, from wherever it had lain hidden for close to thirty years, a vivid image of the picture on which his dream was based flashed back into the forefront of his mind.

'Our old nanny—she'd been with my father so she really was quite old, not just old to small children— had a picture in a frame. It showed a little thatched cottage, with roses over the door, and hollyhocks standing straight and tall beside the wall. Flowers everywhere, probably a bird or two. But somehow I always felt, if I could open that front door—it was blue—inside I'd find a family. Mother in the kitchen, father and dog by the fire, small children at the table while a rosy-cheeked baby crawled across the floor. The image of what was behind that door was so clear to me, I finally realised it must have been another picture I'd once seen—maybe on a calendar in Nanny's room as well. It was the kind of sentimental tripe she adored.'

'Tripe? When it made such an impression on you?'

Maggie had stopped the car and she turned to look at him.

'Even a novice in psychoanalysis, knowing how you grew up, would be able to explain all that to you.'

She reached over and touched his shoulder.

'I think it's sweet. Like me and the farm and a bedroom of my own! I guess all kids have dreams. But *now*, Phil Park—what does the word home mean to you now?'

She hoped she sounded casual enough, asking this question, but this 'home and hearth' Phil didn't square with the playboy who flirted shamelessly and dated women as casually as she changed her clothes. And given her current state, it would be good to know which was the real Phil. So, although she'd brought up the subject of home to divert him from thinking of the situation with the sick baby, now they were talking it had turned into a good idea.

'I suppose it's wherever I'm living at the time—though none of the places I've been lately have felt like home because I've always known they were temporary arrangements. First in the US, where I started with Alex at one hospital then moved to another, then Melbourne, now here. I can feel at home just about anywhere, I suppose, but...'

He turned to look directly at her, and she knew he was about to share another bit of himself with her. This, she knew, was special, because in the nearly eight months she'd worked with Phil, she'd learned little of him, apart from an apparent attraction to blondes.

'A little bit of that corny thatched cottage is embedded deep in my subconscious. If I think at all of marriage—hypothetically, of course—I find myself reverting to a modern-day version of that particular picture. Myself in a chair by the fire—children chattering around the place—pets to pat—a wife in the kitchen. Totally unacceptable view in this enlightened day and age of equal rights and careers for women, I know, but the idea persists. I suppose because my parents' marriage *wasn't* like that—my mother lived her own life based mainly on good works, my father was always away—and it was such a disaster, I have this conviction that only something drastically different would work.'

He gave a huff of laughter—at himself, Maggie knew—but she also knew this was very real to him, and given his upbringing she could understand why he saw this dream as an ideal.

Diametrically opposite from her ideal but, then, it would be, she thought gloomily. That was the way life worked!

'I suppose the wife slaving in the kitchen is a blonde?' she heard herself ask, and hoped she didn't sound as bitchy as she must be feeling to have said it in the first place.

Fortunately Phil took it well, laughing as he opened the car door and began unloading the shopping bags.

'At least you stereotyped yourself, offering to do the cooking,' he reminded her. 'You can't blame me for that.'

'I will cook because I enjoy it,' Maggie told him haughtily, 'not because I'm a woman.'

Phil laughed again, then unlocked the back door, freeing a delighted Minnie who leapt about his legs with yaps of excitement before heading for Maggie to welcome her home.

'There's that damn word again,' she muttered to herself, half wishing she hadn't been so persistent in her questioning.

Phil dumped his load of groceries on the kitchen table, and began to unpack them, stacking things into the pantry or fridge. The woman in his childhood dream kitchen *had* been a blonde, but watching Maggie bustling about in this real kitchen was far more seductive than any dream.

'I think I'll go up to the hospital and see if I can see

the baby,' he said, as she stacked things on the bench beneath the window, apparently in readiness for some dish she was about to prepare.

She spun towards him.

'See Dr Ellis? Ask to see the baby?'

Phil shook his head.

'I doubt Ellis is still there. My bet is he's passed it back to the paediatrician. The baby will be in the SBCU—no, that's English, and PICU is American—special care unit you call it here, don't you?'

'We all understand PICU to be Paediatric Intensive Care Unit so stick with that. Yes, the baby will be there. So what?'

'So most of the intensivists we have working in our PICU also work in that one, and I know them all, so I'd like to take a peek at the notes and look at the scans. I imagine they did two-dimensional and Doppler echocardiography. A lot of these cases are associated with hypoblastic left heart syndrome—meaning the child has virtually no left ventricle. We can operate to help his heart function without one, but there again the mortality rate is high unless it's done as a carefully staged procedure—three stages to it—when the child is older.'

He pushed his hair back off his forehead—he had to get a haircut some time soon—and shook his head and sighed.

'I don't really know why I want to go up there, Maggie, just that I do. I can't get that baby out of my mind.'

Maggie shifted some of the things she'd put on the bench into the fridge.

'I'll come with you.'

He had to smile.

'To see the baby or be my support person?' he teased, then realised she wasn't smiling.

'I'll come because you're likely to decide that maybe there *is* something you can do for him, and if you operate, or opt to assist someone else to operate, then you'll need the best paediatric anaesthetist available in this hospital, and that's me.'

'Modest little thing, aren't you?' he said, as she ducked past him towards the front door.

'Not falsely so,' she said, turning to smile. 'But that's my goal—to be the best, not only in this hospital but in Australia, and after Australia the world. And I'll get there, too. I don't think it's boasting when we say things like that. We all know our limitations but surely we should also know our abilities as well, and be confident of them?'

And though he'd been seduced earlier by Maggie's domesticity in the kitchen, he now remembered other things he knew of her. Maggie was a career-woman through and through. In fact, her determination to learn all she could from working with Alex, and the expertise she had already developed anaesthetising neonates and very small infants, was what had persuaded Alex to bring her to Sydney as a member of the team.

'Would you give up work and be a stay-at-home mum if you had a baby?' he asked, as they set off to walk the short distance to the hospital.

She stopped dead, so suddenly he thought at first she must have turned an ankle or injured herself in some other way.

'Are you OK?'

'Of course I am,' she muttered at him, striding along again. 'But we're talking operations, and suddenly you're asking if I'd stop work to have a baby. Not that it's any of your business, but the answer's no. I've done as many years of training as you have—well, not quite as many because you're older. I'm a specialist with skills that go beyond those of general anaesthetics, skills I intend to keep improving and honing. Turn that question around. Would you stop work if you had a baby?'

'Good point,' he said easily, trying to regain some lost ground, but he knew the companionable ease they'd shared earlier was gone. Her voice could have scythed through bamboo! And he'd guessed that was how Maggie would feel, even though he couldn't re-member motherhood and families coming up in pre-vious discussions, so why had he been stupid enough to ask the question?

Surely not because of one night in bed with a col-league and a vague memory of a stupid childhood dream!

'If they have decided to go ahead with the operation, will you offer to assist?'

He glanced her way, wondering if she really wanted to know or if it was just her way of getting the con-versation back on medical matters. The full lips that had figured in his dreams of late were set in a tight line, so he guessed it was a deliberate conversational shift.

He accepted it, thinking through his reply.

'I don't know,' he told her honestly. 'It's a matter of what's been decided. And it will depend on the sur-geon. He—or she—may not want me there. Scott Douglas is the senior cardiac surgical registrar, and he's assisted at a lot of our ops. He's a terrific surgeon, lacking some experience of infants and neonates but getting there.'

Then something else struck him.

'Will you offer?'

She turned and smiled at him.

'It's a baby so, yes, of course I will. I'm lucky in that the decision to operate isn't mine, but my special skill is in giving the little one the best possible chance during and immediately after the op.'

She was silent for a moment, then she added, 'The best possible chance!' in a voice so soft he barely heard it, and shook her head as if to chase some persistent thought away.

CHAPTER FOUR

THE first person they saw in the PICU was Rachel, the theatre sister who was part of their team.

'My guess is they're going to operate,' Maggie whispered to Phil, who nodded, his face set in an unreadable mask.

'Glad you guys are here,' Rachel greeted them. 'Someone from the hospital phoned Kurt and, thinking it meant Phil had a surgical patient, I tagged along. Now it seems someone else is operating. Kurt went through to Theatre—our theatre—to check his machine, but I don't know if they'll need me.'

She shrugged her shoulders and nodded towards one of the glass-walled rooms where a group of men and women was clustered around a crib.

'You doing the anaesthetic?' she asked Maggie, who looked from the group to Phil, her mind racing.

Although he'd said little, she knew he was still fretting over his decision. Would her going into Theatre with the other group seem like a betrayal?

Worse, how would he feel, definitely on the outside, while all his colleagues on the team were involved?

Purely for the sake of solidarity, should she refuse to help if asked?

'If they ask me to assist, I will,' she said, knowing her own ethical standards would dictate that choice, although her heart would have preferred to stand by Phil.

He nodded as if he understood, but his lips were tight in his grim white face.

She was asked to assist only minutes later, by Scott Douglas, who looked as haunted by what was going on as she felt.

'Phil,' he said, but spoke too hesitantly, for Phil had turned away and was walking not towards their rooms but to the lifts. Leaving the hospital—cutting himself off from them.

From her...

Routine took over, and she moved to the theatre complex, changing into theatre pyjamas then checking all the equipment and assembling the drugs and fluids she'd need.

A tall lanky man came in and introduced himself as Evan Knowles.

'I do this stuff over at the Kids, normally, but when one of the surgeons was called over here he asked me to come along.'

'Is he good?' Maggie asked, stepping back so Evan could familiarise himself with things in the near-new theatre.

'I try not to think about what the surgeons are doing and focus solely on what's happening with the patient.'

He smiled at Maggie, and added, 'To tell the truth, I'm not one hundred per cent certain about how much interference we should run on neonates and infants— how much gross surgical trauma they should have to endure. I've read a lot of studies on measuring pain in them and that's really where I'd like to go—long-term effects of pain in babies and children. Maybe there's none, but we tend to think about all the other things, like the possibility of brain damage and stroke—yet you and I both know, having managed pain in patients in Intensive Care, just how little we know about it in babies.'

Maggie warmed to the man who spoke so openly about his doubt, and, watching him check what she had ready, she felt confident he was a good anaesthetist.

Maybe she could slip away, join Phil at—at Alex's house.

'You will stay?' Evan asked, apparently picking up the thought in the air.

'Yes, I'll stay.'

It was a long and traumatic afternoon. The baby boy arrested on the operating table, and the shock cart was brought close to shock his heart back to action. Then the small heart was so badly deformed it seemed any kind of surgical intervention would be impossible, yet the surgeon did what he could, Scott and Rachel both helping. Rachel, who for years had worked with Alex, and in the US was known as a physician's assistant, seemed to know as much as either of the surgeons.

The first stage was to insert the cannulae, which would run his blood through the bypass machine, but the arteries and veins were so tiny it was a Herculean effort to get the plastic tubes into place.

The baby arrested again, Rachel reacting first, taking the base of the little heart in her fingers and gently squeezing it, keeping blood flowing to the baby's brain until he could be hooked up to the machine. Then Kurt had a problem getting the blood flow pressure low enough for the baby's vessels to handle it and yet sufficiently high to keep the little body perfused.

'This is not going to work,' Evan whispered to Maggie, who was reading out the temperature figures as the machine cooled the blood.

'I thought you didn't watch,' she whispered back.

'I don't,' Evan told her, 'but look at the monitor. Look at the blood acidity reading. If he arrests again— and he will—we won't be able to do anything.'

Maggie looked towards the tiny mortal on the table, so little of him in view, and her own pulse rate accelerated as fear clutched at her heart. What if it had been her child?

What choice would she make?

Operate on the slim chance he or she might survive?

'We'll get him through,' she said fiercely to Evan. 'We can fix acidity—we can fix anything!'

She was aware of his eyes, a nice grey colour, studying her, as if trying to make out what had brought on this sudden determination, then he said, 'Whatever!' and turned back towards the monitor.

Maybe she'd have to get out of this field, she thought, once again pressing her hand to her stomach. But even thinking such a thing worried her. She'd always been able to separate her work and personal selves—always been able to focus solely on work when she was working, even to the extent that she barely gave Phil a glance when he was in Theatre with her.

Well, maybe she did give him the odd glance, but she didn't, when in Theatre, think the lascivious thoughts about him that were likely to pop into her head outside the hospital world!

So all she had to do was to divorce the baby-carrying Maggie from the hospital one, and she'd be fine.

The operation dragged on. The tiny heart was stopped with cardioplegia, so the surgeons could open it up to fix the valves, but because its effect was only temporary, more had to be given after twenty minutes—the timing critical. Everyone was aware of the time, everyone knowing that the longer it stretched, the less chance this baby had of surviving.

Finally, he was taken off the bypass machine and his heart was stimulated, but the little organ refused to beat. Evan bagged the baby, forcing air into his lungs, while the surgeon's hands tried to stimulate the heart into beating.

Collective breaths were held, the air still with a dread anticipation.

'Shock again,' the surgeon ordered, but once again it was Rachel who saw the action.

'No, it's beating,' she said, and Maggie turned to the images on the wall-screens and saw the tiny, stitched heart valiantly pumping.

She had to blink away a tear, and swallow a lump that had risen in her throat.

Good thing the more observant team members weren't around—they'd have caught her out for sure, and her 'ice-cool Maggie' image would have been shattered for ever.

'Do you always get emotional?' Evan asked, and she realised she'd been sprung anyway.

'Hardly ever,' she told him, bringing the hospital Maggie back into place. 'Almost never.'

'I think it's OK to feel something,' Evan said. 'After all, these are babies you're dealing with, and being a woman you must feel some tie.'

Maggie contemplated kicking him hard on his ankle, but decided against it. He was probably only voicing a thought that ninety-nine per cent of men would voice—or at least think—in similar circumstances.

'Six hours—not too bad,' the surgeon said, finally stepping back from the table and letting Scott close the wound.

Maggie heard Kurt mutter something about the time on bypass, and knew he was worried about possible brain or kidney damage to the child. Anyone who had ever worked with Alex knew his feelings about not doing more harm than good, and he was adamant that too long on the bypass machine fell into the 'harm' category.

Rachel was assisting Scott now, explaining to him why Alex was fussy about the way the tubes and drains and wires were taped.

'It makes it more comfortable for the baby,' she said, 'and a comfortable baby recovers faster.'

'Does Dr Attwood do that with all his infants?' Evan asked, as he watched the procedure. 'Has he ever done any studies on measuring their post-operative comfort—things like pain levels?'

'I don't know about the post-op studies, but he swears post-operative care is just as important as the surgery.'

'Well, that must include post-op pain relief. I need to talk to this man. Where is he?'

'On his honeymoon,' Rachel told him, and gave a little laugh that sounded forced.

Had Rachel had a soft spot for the man with whom she worked so closely? Maggie had never considered it before, assuming, since Rachel and Kurt lived together, that they were a couple.

But she and Phil were now living together, and they certainly weren't a couple.

She shut her mind to these stray thoughts, upset to find her other self intruding yet again at the hospital.

'He's all yours now,' Scott said, and Maggie turned to Evan.

'I guess he's all yours really. You're the person called in.'

'But you're the local,' he said. 'You'll be seeing him in hospital. I guess we should share him.'

'He's arrested again,' Rachel said quietly, and the other theatre sister wheeled the crash cart back close to the baby, while the circulating nurse pressed the alarm button for the surgeon to return.

Surgeons pulled on gloves, the wound was reopened, the baby shocked again. Maggie injected drugs into his veins as the surgeon ordered them, her fingers trembling as she measured out the doses, her heart clinging to hope.

Muttered curses, demands, frantic, dramatic measures to save an infant who'd been born with the odds against him from the start—every member of the team rigid with tension as they willed him to survive.

Babies born with such huge problems die, Maggie reminded herself, but she desperately wanted this one to live.

For Phil's sake so he wouldn't feel badly later.

For her own, because she knew it could have been her baby...

But no amount of stimulation would bring him back and as they left the theatre, for reasons more to do with the stresses of the morning and the long hours in Theatre than her own condition, Maggie found tears sliding down her cheeks.

So she did cry for these babies, she realised, wiping them angrily away before Evan, or anyone else, saw them. But it was too late. The tall man had hooked his arm around her shoulder and drawn her close, and she put her head against his chest and cried for all the babies they couldn't save.

And cried for Phil, who would be devastated but, she guessed, would never cry...

'Very touching,' a cool voice said, and Maggie jerked away from the comfort of Evan's arms to see the man she cried for standing only feet away from them.

'The baby died,' Maggie said bleakly, then realised from the set expression on Phil's face she'd get no sympathy from him.

She got her confirmation in the shrug he gave as he walked towards their rooms.

'Boyfriend?' Evan asked, and Maggie shook her head.

'Colleague,' she explained, but didn't elaborate. Evan would go back to his hospital and get on with his life, while she and Phil would continue to work and live together.

The problem was, she'd get over the death of this baby far more easily than Phil would, for the demons that drove him would always be questioning whether he could have done better—could have saved the tiny boy's life.

She said goodbye to Evan, and was heading for the suite herself, needing a coffee and sugar jolt and a chance to unwind, when he called her back.

'Hey, don't rush off without telling me where I can get a decent cup of coffee around this place. Don't you guys have somewhere you unwind?'

They did, of course, but she had a feeling the atmosphere in the suite of rooms, with Phil there, wouldn't be very conducive to unwinding. More likely they'd get wound even tighter.

'There's the canteen,' she began dubiously, then heard Phil's voice again.

'For heaven's sake, Maggie, take the man into the suite and give him a real cup of coffee. I'm leaving, so you needn't worry about me getting in the way.'

He stalked past them and Maggie watched him go, seeing anger and something else in the stiff set of his shoulders and the swift strides he took.

'They asked him to do the op,' she explained to Evan as she led him into their rooms. 'He believed the baby was too young—that the operation had more chance of success in a month. Statistically, it's true, apparently.'

'Well, the baby died so maybe he feels justified.'

Maggie swung towards her companion, unable to believe he could have meant what he'd just said.

'I hope I'd never feel a baby's death was justification for one of my decisions,' she snapped, and Evan held up his hands.

'Hey, I phrased that badly. Don't jump all over me.' He peered down at her. 'Sure he's not your boyfriend?'

She didn't answer, fussing with the coffee-machine, and he continued, 'All I meant was that he's now been proved right. You're correct in saying it's a terrible way to be proved right, but he was, wasn't he?'

Maggie knew where he was coming from and nodded.

'But I don't for a moment think Phil will see it that way. His torment will be whether he could have done it better, and whether, by refusing to do it, he signed the baby's death warrant.'

'But that's like playing God,' Evan protested, accepting the cup of coffee and adding three sugars to it. 'Assuming you'd do better!'

'This is a stupid conversation,' Maggie said crossly. 'Phil's the last person who'd do a "playing God" routine, but he wouldn't be human if he didn't have some what-if questions rattling in his head.'

She stirred her coffee and shifted the conversation to Evan's work at the Children's hospital, asking about staffing and working conditions, general questions that couldn't possibly lead to an argument.

'Do you realise how late it is?' Evan said some time later. 'As neither of us have eaten, how about we grab a bite somewhere?'

Maggie felt and heard her stomach gurgle obligingly at the mention of food and looked at her watch. It was after nine, far too late to prepare the meal she'd planned for herself and Phil. And by now he was sure to have eaten. Hadn't he said he and Alex, when alone in the house, did their own thing?

'Good idea,' she told Evan, thinking of the added benefit of putting off going home so she wouldn't have to discuss what had happened in Theatre. 'You have a choice of Thai or Italian restaurants within walking distance. I like both so you choose.'

Evan chose the Italian but insisted on driving, although it was only a short distance. Over the meal, they talked shop, Evan expanding on some studies he'd done and what he'd like to do.

'You're probably aware that not so long ago, people believed neonates and infants didn't feel pain, and as recently as 1995 a study showed not all anaesthetists used pain relief during an operation.'

'It depends on the relief and the age of the child,' Maggie said. 'I'm wary of using opioids on premmie babies, but on most infants I use a cocktail of morphine, codeine and fentanyl for pain. I wonder if it's because babies seem to recover so well from really major surgery that we believe they either don't feel pain as much as adults or don't know what it is so it isn't a negative in their recovery.'

She finished her glass of wine and sat back in her chair, suddenly exhausted.

'I really should get going. Tomorrow's a workday and I only shifted house this morning and haven't settled properly in.'

'I could help you settle in,' Evan said, and Maggie caught the suggestiveness beneath the words.

She smiled at him.

'I think I can manage on my own.'

'Fair enough,' he said easily, 'but I'd like it put on record I'm single, uncommitted to anyone at the moment, disease-free and attracted to you. Any chance we might see each other again?'

Maggie hesitated. She'd had a pleasant evening, and had relaxed enough to enjoy Evan's company, but...

'You're seeing someone?'

She looked into his clear grey eyes and couldn't tell a lie.

'No,' she said, 'but I'm a bit up in the air at the moment. I haven't been in Sydney long, and I've just moved house for the third time in two months...'

'It doesn't have to be anything hot or heavy,' Evan said, picking up on her uncertainty. 'A few casual dates to see where things might go—you said you liked dancing, I do too—and I could take you to some great dance places in Sydney. You like the salsa?'

Maggie did and couldn't deny it, so she smiled at him.

'Maybe when I've settled in,' she said, as Evan signalled for a waiter then insisted on paying for their meal.

'I asked you to eat with me,' he reminded her, when she argued.

He drove her the short distance back to Alex's house, where lights downstairs told her nothing. Phil could be down there reading or watching TV—she realised she had no idea what Phil did in his spare time—or he could be out and have left the lights on for her.

'I'll see you to the door,' Evan said, opening his car door.

'Really, there's no need,' Maggie told him, realising she'd never got the key Alex had said he was going to leave for her at the house, and if the front door was locked she'd have to ring the doorbell.

And hope Phil *wasn't* out.

But having Phil open the door to find her and Evan standing there wasn't an appealing prospect either.

She hesitated, but Evan showed no sign of leaving, and by now Minnie had realised someone was outside and was doing a fierce watchdog imitation, yapping furiously from inside.

The door opened before Maggie could make a decision, and Phil stood there, the light behind him throwing his face into shadow.

'Forget your key?'

'Forgot to pick one up. Did you meet Evan properly? Evan Knowles, anaesthetist from the Children's. Evan, this is Phil Park.'

She managed the introduction, watched the two men shake hands—an awkward move for Phil who had quietened Minnie by lifting her into the crook of his left arm—then turned to Evan and offered her own.

'Nice to have met you and thanks for dinner. I'd be

pleased to hear more about your pain studies some time.'

She shook his hand formally, and hoped he get the message this was not the time to say something personal. Not that there was anything between her and Phil—apart from that one night and a pregnancy—but the tension in the air suggested something different.

Something possessive?

Surely not. For all Phil's talk of rose-bowered cottages and domestically devoted families, his dating behaviour suggested he was more a 'why buy a book when you can join a library' man, too scared of commitment to go out with any woman more than once or twice.

'Knowles,' he had growled in acknowledgement of the introduction, then he remained standing in the doorway, glowering like a cloud looking for a parade on which to rain.

'I'll give you a call,' Evan said, then to Maggie's surprise, he leant forward and kissed her on the cheek.

'Quick worker!' Phil muttered, while Maggie watched Evan walk down the path and through the gate—shutting it carefully behind him—then to his car.

Maggie contemplated pointing out to Phil that it was none of his business, then decided she had no desire to continue the conversation. She stepped forward, intending to move past him and up the stairs to her room, but he was too quick, shutting the door and setting Minnie down on the floor, then grasping Maggie's arm.

'But he hasn't a clue how to kiss a woman goodnight, has he?'

He swung her around and, before she had any idea of what he intended, his head descended then his lips claimed hers, so fiercely demanding she had to grasp his shoulder to remain upright.

Don't kiss him back!

The warning sounded somewhere in her head but it obviously didn't penetrate to her lips which were clinging to his, not only responding but making demands of their own.

For a few minutes Maggie managed to remain detached so she felt like an onlooker watching this passionate embrace from afar, then the heat the kiss was generating took control and her mind ceased to function.

Minnie saved the day—or night!—her hysterical noise finally penetrating Maggie's consciousness enough for her to pull away from Phil.

'Does she want to go outside?' she asked, too breathless to do anything more than mumble the words.

'She can get outside through the hatch in the back door,' Phil said, and Maggie was pleased to hear his usually precise voice was also a little strangled.

'I'll take her through,' Maggie said, bending to lift the little dog into her arms.

'Thank you,' she whispered when they were out of earshot. She pressed a kiss on the dog's soft downy head.

By the time she returned, Phil was gone, so she turned out the downstairs lights and went up to bed.

Alone.

Though she had doubts that would have been the case had the hot kiss continued any longer...

Agreeing to Alex's request that Maggie move in was obviously the worst thing he'd ever done, Phil decided as he tossed and turned in his bed that night. As if he hadn't had a bad enough day, with the decision not to operate and then the baby's death, then seeing Maggie with that lanky anaesthetist—first crying in his arms, then coming home so late they *had* to have been out to dinner together.

But you didn't need to kiss her, his picky conscience said.

No? libido replied. When that long skinny streak of misery had just pecked her on the cheek? Someone had to show her what a real kiss felt like!

Did you a lot of good! a new voice muttered, and Phil, tired of listening to voices in his head, listened instead for noises in the house. Noises that suggested Maggie might be on her way up to bed.

Alone!

It was better this way—that wasn't a voice, it was common sense, of which he had apparently retained a few shreds.

But his body didn't believe what common sense had suggested. His body longed to once again have Maggie's body tucked against it.

And not just for sex, though he'd be a liar if he said that didn't come into it.

Sure he wouldn't sleep, he counted sutures, spacing them just the right distance apart, and woke to daylight and someone tapping on his door.

'Come!'

The door opened a crack and Maggie peered dubiously inside.

'It's OK, I'm decent,' he assured her, pulling up the sheet to hide his bare chest, although on that one memorable night she'd seen more of his skin than that of his upper torso.

She edged into the room but only far enough for him to see the whole person rather than just the head.

'I'm on my way to work and I wasn't sure if you wanted to be woken. If you were called out during the night and trying to catch up on some sleep, I'm sorry, but I slept in myself and wondered if you might have done the same.'

Maggie sounded so flustered Phil checked to see he was decently covered. His sheet had become untucked, so his feet were poking out the bottom, but unless Maggie had a thing for feet, he couldn't see anything to embarrass her.

Damn! It must be the kiss. How could he have been so stupid? Only yesterday he'd decided how nice it would be to have Maggie as a housemate, then he'd blown the platonic colleague scenario to bits with his behaviour.

'Well, as long as you're awake, I'll be going,' Maggie was saying, still flustered he could tell, but apparently it was by his feet as that was where her gaze had been directed.

Hmm! Turned on by toes? libido wondered, but the real Phil slapped him down.

'Thanks for waking me,' he said. 'I doubt if anyone will be looking for me, but if they are, tell them I'll be there in half an hour.'

As he spoke, memories of the events—the medical events—of the previous day came rushing back, and the depression he'd managed to keep at bay with thoughts of kissing Maggie returned in full force.

'OK, I'll see you later,' Maggie said, and she fled down the stairs, one hand against her stomach as she made silent apologies to her baby.

It was Phil's fault—firstly because he'd slept in and

she'd had to go into his bedroom. Then for leaving his feet on show. Pale, slim, really elegant feet, with straight, well-manicured toes. Except that the second toe was longer than the big toe and Maggie had a sudden image of her baby, not nearly up to growing toes as yet, being born with the same distinctive feet—slim and elegant, with the second toe longer than the first.

As if it mattered what her baby's feet were like, she scolded herself as she hurried up the road to work—hurrying not because she was late but to put physical distance between herself and Phil.

Had she had strange thoughts flipping in and out of her head during her previous pregnancies?

Pregnancy, singular. She hadn't known about the first until she'd had her second miscarriage and had realised she'd been through it before.

And as for toes, in planned pregnancies, most women would have done some genetic comparisons with the baby's father, and toes were almost sure to have come up in conversation.

CHAPTER FIVE

'AND what are you so deep in thought about?'

Maggie came back to earth to find Rachel standing just inside the gate that led into the hospital grounds.

'Toes!' Maggie told her, smiling when she saw Rachel's surprise.

Her colleague shrugged and said, 'As good a subject for contemplation as any other on a Monday morning,' then linked her arm through Maggie's and continued towards the hospital.

The gesture put all thoughts of toes out of Maggie's head. Rachel had never sought her out before, yet today it seemed as if she'd been waiting for her.

The events of the previous day—the loss of the baby—came flooding back. If the usually super-confident Rachel had felt in need of a little moral support to walk back into the hospital this morning, how much worse must Phil be feeling? Maggie wondered.

Not that Phil would appreciate someone pandering to him, but the questions that had bedevilled him the previous day must still be racing around in his head.

Which would explain his strange behaviour with the kiss. It had been a release of physical tension, nothing more.

'Maggie, you're wanted in the cath lab,' Becky Myles, their unit secretary, said when she walked in. 'Neonate with pulmonary stenosis.'

Maggie dropped her handbag into a desk drawer and grabbed her coat. The catheterisation lab was just off the adult ICU, a room with a big glass window behind which the technician sat, talking through a microphone to the medical staff and controlling the huge X-ray machine that hung above the operating table. Pictures from the machine were visible on screens on the wall, so the person performing the procedure, which entailed passing a wire from the groin of the patient up into the heart, could see where the wire was going.

Babies were sedated before the procedure to keep them still, and with newborns the amount of sedation was critical, which was why the cardiologist had called Maggie in.

'The echo shows a problem with the pulmonary artery valve so blood's building up in the right ventricle instead of heading for the lungs,' the woman cardiologist told Maggie. 'I can usually open it with a balloon—it's a temporary measure but saves operating on a neonate.'

Maggie intubated the baby carefully, mentally apologising to the tiny scrap of humanity for the things she was doing to her. She wondered whether the cardiologist's words had a hidden meaning, whether the woman had heard of Phil's refusal to operate, though this was a different problem—or the same problem, but with the valves in a different artery.

Maggie watched the baby, worried about the rising blood gas levels, then glanced at a screen to see the wire inching up the blood vessel towards the heart. Once the wire reached its destination, a hollow tube would be slipped over it and the wire withdrawn, then a tiny balloon on the end of the tube would be inflated with water forced down the tube, and the inflating balloon should force the valves open.

It was delicate, precise work, with risks all along the way.

Maggie knew crossing her fingers wasn't going to make a scrap of difference, but she did it anyway.

Phil was walking up the street, considering whether there was any feasible way he could move from Alex's house and so escape life with Maggie, when his pager vibrated in his pocket.

'Hospital! Well, I'm nearly there,' he said, only realising he'd spoken aloud when two boys on their way to school walked carefully around him.

He picked up his speed, striding now, wondering what lay ahead of him this morning. At least thinking about escaping life with Maggie had stopped him thinking about yesterday's disaster.

Jenny Payne, the staff paediatric cardiologist, met him near the ICU.

'Newborn with a huge heart murmur—the echo shows a faulty valve on the pulmonary artery. I catheterised her to try to open it with a balloon, but it won't open,' she explained, handing him the case notes—a thickish file already, although the baby was only hours old.

Déjà vu! Phil thought. Another balloon valvuplasty that didn't work.

'Let me check these and talk to Becky. We have a four-year-old booked in for a first-stage repair of a tetralogy of Fallot, but there's no reason we can't delay that slightly and do the baby first.'

'You'll do the baby?'

Phil closed his eyes for a moment and told himself to remain calm.

'Jenny, the baby needs a shunt put in to get blood

from her heart to her lungs. Of course I'll do it. We've done three or four in the time we've been here. Why wouldn't I do it?'

She looked embarrassed, as well she might, and Phil took pity on her.

'A shunt is a minor op to keep the baby going until we can do a more complete repair. What Dr Ellis—I assume you've heard about the argument I had with him yesterday that you're looking so jittery?—wanted was a different matter altogether. He wanted me to do major surgery of a kind that has been proved to be more successful when the infant's older.'

'I know that,' Jenny said, 'and I should have known better than to listen to the stories Ellis has been circulating, but he's a dangerous enemy to have, Phil, so watch your step.'

Something else to keep his mind off Maggie, Phil told himself as he took the notes to the ICU desk, spread them out and looked at what they knew so far about Baby Creagh.

The team would already be preparing for the tet but if Maggie hadn't done the pre-med on their patient, a stalwart little boy called Pete, they could do the baby first.

He bundled up the notes and headed for their rooms, finding Becky there and alerting her to the change in schedule. She paged Maggie first, then Rachel, who would tell the others.

'We won't need Kurt for this first one,' Phil told her, as the phone rang on her desk.

Becky nodded and spoke into the phone.

'Maggie's on her way,' she said to Phil as she put down the receiver then lifted it again as the second page was answered.

Phil nodded and, notes in hand, left the rooms. He was at the sink in the theatre suite, scrubbing furiously at his arms, when Maggie came in. The hospital Maggie, all dedication and efficiency! He could handle this.

'I did the anaesthetic on Baby Creagh when Jenny did the cath. We had to use bicarb to neutralise acidosis even in such a short procedure. I'll have it on hand but be prepared for fibrillation if she's still unstable.'

Phil turned towards her, holding his dripping hands high in the air.

'Thanks, Mags,' he said. 'We'll watch it.'

And though this was the hospital Maggie he was talking to, he couldn't help but notice anxiety in her soft dark eyes and a tightness in her usually full and luscious lips.

Hospital Maggie with full and luscious lips? He was definitely losing his grip.

But the tightness bothered him more than his reaction.

'Are you all right? Are you still thinking about yesterday?'

The lips flashed into a smile.

'Depends what bit of yesterday you mean!' she said cheekily, then she darted off, leaving him wondering if she could possibly have meant the kiss.

And if so, did that mean she might consider resuming a relationship with him?

'Gore-tex shunt?'

He turned, arms still dripping water, to find Rachel hovering behind him.

'I'm sorry, what did you ask?'

'Nothing complicated,' she said with a smile. 'Just wondering if you'll use a Gore-tex shunt or do you want to try one of the new ones that rep brought in the other day? The information he had on them and recommendations from surgeons back home all sounded good.'

Pleased to be able to focus on work, Phil considered the question. The new shunts had also been demonstrated at a conference he'd attended recently and looked good.

'Put a range of both out and we'll see. It would be good if we can find one of either make that is the exact size.'

From the beginning of his time with Alex, he had learned the importance of doing the little things right. He explained this to Scott a little later, when Scott had made an incision, not midline, but a small cut between two ribs on the side of the baby's chest.

'We're already invading this infant's body and putting in something that doesn't belong there, so the least we can do is make it the right size, put it in the right place and cause minimum disruption to the proper pattern of her blood vessels.'

With the light angled so he could see into the small hole they'd made, he inserted probes into an artery and a vein to keep an eye on the pressure in each, then carefully clamped the baby's subclavian artery, cut a small nick, and with swift but careful stitches sewed the shunt into place. Then did the same thing with the pulmonary artery, attaching the little tube with precision. Blood would now bypass the blocked valves and be shunted into the lungs of the baby, picking up oxygen there and bringing it back to the heart to be circulated through the body.

Maggie's report showed all was well, and Phil felt a huge sense of relief, although this was little more than a minor procedure compared with what he would be doing later.

'There, that should hold her for a while,' he said. 'When she's a bit older—eighteen months, if she can make it that far—we'll give her a new valve and remove the shunt. There's a lot of work being done now on replacing aortic valves with working pulmonary valves and putting a new man-made valve in the pulmonary artery, which takes less pressure so the valve doesn't need to be as strong. They do it a lot on adults but it's still experimental with children, although lab tests suggest the transferred valve will grow with the child and save more surgery later on.'

Scott shook his head.

'I can't believe the stuff I'm learning from you and Alex.'

'Make the most of it,' Phil told him. 'I'm still learning but Alex is one of the best there is. And learn from Rachel, too—you won't find a better theatre assistant than her anywhere. It's my belief she could do my job as well as I can, if not better.'

The atmosphere was suddenly light-hearted, Rachel giving a huff of laughter and tension Phil hadn't known he'd been feeling draining from his body.

'OK, crew, take a break and be back in…'

He turned to Maggie, knowing she'd need to see young Pete before he came to Theatre.

'When?'

'Better give me an hour—I want to keep an eye on this baby for a while, then make sure there's a nurse available to sit with her. After that, there's pre-med for Pete. Yes, an hour. We'll still only be about forty-five minutes later than we'd originally scheduled.'

Maggie hoped she sounded more together than she

felt. The tension in Theatre when the operation had begun had suggested everyone had heard the stories Dr Ellis had spread. The worst of these was that Phil had choked—refused to do the operation because he'd been afraid he'd fail. No mention of the age of the baby or the statistics that backed up his decision not to operate.

So all the unit members had been on edge and the theatre had seemed to vibrate with tense expectations.

But Baby Creagh was fine, the operation to insert the shunt successful—although once again Maggie found herself surreptitiously crossing her fingers.

She uncrossed them and patted her stomach, telling the multiplying cells in there it must be their fault she was doing such foolish things. At least, she hoped it was the hormone havoc they were creating within her, not a symptom of something more permanent.

She walked with the baby back to the ICU, although she didn't expect her to be in there long. She hooked her up to the in-room ventilator and monitor, checked her blood saturation levels then stood and watched the infant until her anxious parents came in.

'Is she feeling any pain?' the mother asked, and Maggie shook her head, though since Evan had spoken of his desire to study pain in infants, she'd begun to wonder just how they could tell.

Stress leading to acidosis in the blood, she supposed. Or maybe brain activity if they had the infant's head wired to a monitor.

But wires might cause their own anxiety in the infant, so how could they tell what they were measuring?

'Are you worried about her?'

The question made her turn from where she'd stopped outside Baby Creagh's room, pondering these things, to face the questioner.

Phil!

'No, she's good. I was thinking about Evan—'

She stopped because unless she wanted to yell her thoughts at Phil's departing back, there was no point in saying anything more. He'd swept away as if summoned to a dire emergency.

Because she'd mentioned Evan's name?

Why should that upset him?

He'd made no attempt to pursue their relationship beyond that one night, so it was obvious it had meant nothing to him—beyond, possibly, a little embarrassment.

So he couldn't be jealous...

Puzzlement turned to anger. Here *she'd* been, feeling sympathetic and supportive towards him, and he'd walked away from her in a huff.

'Well, he can stay huffy,' she muttered to herself, making her way back to the rooms for a coffee before seeing little Pete to prepare him for the lengthy operation that lay ahead of him.

She walked into the rooms to find Phil there, with a surgeon from the Children's who'd assisted Alex in an operation some weeks ago, and, of all people, Evan Knowles.

Maggie greeted them politely, made herself coffee, then excused herself, explaining she had work to do. She supposed it was inevitable Evan would follow her out.

'When Phil asked Dave to assist, he—Dave, that is—asked me if I'd like to come along. I haven't seen a tet repair and he knew I'd be interested.'

'It's a complex procedure,' Maggie told him, 'and long, because there's so much that has to be repaired— the pulmonary valves, shifting the aorta, fixing whatever holes there are between the atria or ventricles. This is just the first stage. Pete will have two more operations after this before his heart can function as normally as possible.'

Evan loped along beside her while she explained this, then she introduced him to the little boy who needed their help to lead a normal life.

'Pete, this is Dr Evan. He's going to help me watch over you while you're asleep.'

Pete extended his hand and gravely shook Evan's, his short, slightly clubbed fingers lost in Evan's big palm.

'How do you do?' Evan said politely, and Maggie gave him full marks for treating this special patient with respect.

She explained to Pete what she was going to give him—'to make you feel a bit sleepy'—and how he would feel when he woke up.

'Dr Evan might visit you again after the operation,' she said, thinking the four-year-old might be able to articulate some of what he was feeling.

'I'd like to do that if it's OK with you,' Evan said, and Pete nodded.

'But Dr Phil will visit me, too?' he asked, anxiety screwing up his little face.

'Of course he will, and so will I. We'll all visit you,' she assured him.

She gave him the syrup that would be quickly absorbed into his bloodstream then unhitched the shunt in his hand from the drip line and got him ready to be moved to Theatre.

His mother had left the hospital earlier, having to see to her other four children, but Pete's father arrived before they took him away.

'How are you going, soldier?' he asked, his voice gruff with concern for his boy.

'Fine, Dad,' Pete managed to say, then Maggie explained she'd already sedated him.

'It's a long procedure, Mr Barron,' she said. 'You could go home and someone can phone you when he's nearly ready to come out.'

The big man shook his head.

'No, I need to be here, near him,' he said. 'I know that sounds stupid because he won't know if I'm here or not, but I've got to stay. My wife, too—she'll be back, just as soon as she's fed the baby and her mother comes to mind the other kids. We're all kinda upset, although we've always known he'd have to have these operations.'

His voice broke as he said the words, and Maggie reached out and touched his shoulder.

'Of course you are,' she said gently, 'but Pete's in the best of hands. No one could do this operation better than the two experts he'll have in there.'

Mr Barron rubbed his hands across his face.

'I know that,' he said, his voice hoarse with emotion. 'I can only thank God for them.'

A nurse arrived to move Pete to Theatre, and Maggie excused herself to go with them. Evan followed her, although she was hardly aware of his presence, her entire being concentrated on what lay ahead of them.

This operation *had* to be successful. For Pete's sake, and for his family's—they were all counting on it. And once again she thought about the burden of responsibility and the pressure family expectations placed on the shoulders of specialists like Alex and Phil.

How did they do it? Day after day, working to save

the lives of children? Knowing full well that one slip and the baby died?

Sometimes they died anyway, and that was another matter. How did they cope with the deaths?

Where in their inner selves were all those dead babies locked away?

'They're in my head, every one of them, and sometimes at night I think I can hear them all crying.'

It was six hours later and Maggie had asked Phil the question. They were sitting on the bed in the on-duty doctors' room of the PICU. Phil would stay the night, getting up at regular intervals to check on Pete, while Maggie was about to leave the hospital but reluctant to go home to an empty house when she was so full of emotion after the operation.

'But what you did today was textbook perfect. Dave said he'd seen Alex do the same op in the US but yours was even more beautiful.'

'Beautiful!' Phil snorted the word. 'We mess around in a small heart and leave it stitched and scarred, and someone calls it beautiful!'

Maggie shifted closer to him, sensing something very like despair in the way he spoke, while his words about the crying babies still echoed in her head and ached heavily in her chest.

'It *is* beautiful when you can take a mistake of nature and fix it so completely it looks as if that's how it always was. Yes, there are sutures and there'll be scar tissue, but when that little boy sits up in bed and smiles at you, and his lips are pink, not blue, won't that still some of the crying in your head? Won't his laughter—and we all know Pete can laugh—give you enough pleasure to cancel out at least one unavoidable death?'

Phil turned towards her.

'You'd think it would, wouldn't you?' he said, sounding so harsh and un-Phil-like she put her arms around him and drew his head down onto her shoulder, holding him tightly to her in an effort to banish his ghosts.

Not a good thing to do from her point of view as her body seemed to think this was a romantic embrace, not a comforting one, but she massaged his shoulders—so tense still—and kneaded her fingers into his scalp.

'Come on,' she teased, 'where's the post-op euphoria we shared after the transplant on Amy? You're usually on a high after an operation. Alex is the one who suffers letdown.'

'If I cheer up you'll stop massaging, and it feels like bliss, Mags,' he said.

'I won't stop,' she promised.

He lifted his head and she saw his eyes were smiling again—for the first time in what seemed like ages.

'You could massage lower down,' he said cheekily, and Maggie felt herself blush for the first time since she'd been fourteen and had walked in on a boy cousin in the shower.

'I only do shoulders on Mondays,' she told him, shifting so there was a space between them, though the air seemed so hot she might as well still have been touching him. 'Turn a bit so I can get at you.'

Phil chuckled and Maggie felt her cheeks heat again, but she ignored the connotation he'd put on her words and dug her fingers into the tight trapezius muscles stretching from his neck and sweeping down across his shoulders.

She remembered how her mother had massaged her neck and shoulders when they'd been tight from studying or working on an assignment on the computer, and wondered if Phil heard the babies crying because there was so much emptiness inside him. Did the crying echo through the spaces that in Maggie's life were filled with the love of her family and the memories of the joy and laughter they'd shared?

He was right about his image of home, whether he'd considered it consciously or not, she thought with a certain degree of bleakness. He needed the security of a stay-at-home wife and a family clustered around his feet, to fill him with the love he'd missed out on in his childhood. Surely then he would no longer hear the babies crying.

'Ouch! Getting a bit rough there.'

Maggie patted the place she'd probably bruised, digging in deeper when she'd realised where her thoughts had led.

'Sorry. Well, you're just about done. I want to check on Pete before I go.'

Phil turned to her again.

'We could both do that then have dinner in the canteen,' he suggested, and though a faint replica of the twinkle remained in his eyes she sensed he needed company and agreed.

And by the end of the meal, when they'd relived the tricky moments of the operation and laughed about the translation difficulties between English English and Australian English, Maggie felt peace had been restored between them and, providing she kept her innermost thoughts and feelings about Phil hidden from view—and her body stopped reacting to every casual touch—they could coexist as housemates in an enjoyable and companionable manner.

'It's dark, I'll walk you home,' Phil said as they were leaving the canteen.

'Don't be silly. It's not far and I've often walked back to Annie's in the dark.'

'I need some fresh clothes anyway,' Phil told her, 'so don't argue.'

He put his arm around her waist and steered her towards the hospital exit.

His touch sent pent-up tremors of excitement flooding through Maggie's body—so much for not reacting. She'd managed to hold lascivious thoughts at bay while she'd massaged him, thinking about the inner man, not his body, but just one touch had let them loose and she wondered if she'd have to revise her opinion about their coexistence!

She moved away from him as soon as they were outside, then shivered in the cold night air.

'You forget it's winter outside when you're shut in the hospital all day,' she complained, pulling a jacket out of her bag and shaking it free of creases.

'Winter!' Phil scoffed, lifting his arms and sniffing the night air. 'You call this winter? Four degrees of frost, a sudden storm that deposits fourteen inches of snow overnight, sleet that cuts into your bones—that's winter. This, Dr Walsh, is nothing more than a bracing summer evening.'

He took her jacket from her and held it while she put it on, then he wrapped it around her and gave her a tight hug.

'That's nothing more than a thanks-for-having-dinner-with-me hug,' he explained, when she stiffened in his arms. 'I had a few demons that needed exorcising and your company helped me do it.'

Ho! Back to coexisting in harmony, Maggie thought.

She might be having licentious thoughts about the man, but he saw her as a colleague, nothing more. Oh, he'd be willing enough to hop into bed with her again—she had no doubt on that score—but for Phil it would mean nothing while for her it would be torment of the worst kind—a tempting taste of what she couldn't have...

Minnie's almost hysterical delight when they opened the front door made Phil feel terrible.

'I should have come down earlier and fed her,' he said, lifting the little dog into his arms and cuddling her. 'Instead of all that navel-gazing you were kind enough to put up with.'

'She's been fed,' Maggie told him. 'I phoned Rod and asked him to come up. He has a key he keeps for the dog-walker so she can get in to collect Minnie each day.'

Phil knew he should have been relieved, but instead felt a contrary dissatisfaction. He could pinpoint it, too. Maggie talking to Rod.

He put Minnie down and took the stairs two at a time, wanting to get clean clothes and get out of the place—if only so his thoughts could fester in peace.

OK, so she'd rung him about the dog—fair enough—but for some weeks he'd harboured the idea that Maggie might be keen on Annie's father, and this chance remark niggled him.

The same way that lanky Evan Knowles irritated him!

Maybe he needed a psychiatrist or psychoanalyst. Someone to sort out his head which, though relatively uncomplicated in the past, had been getting some very strange ideas lately.

He chose clean clothes, packed them in a small overnight bag, put toiletries in with them then headed back downstairs.

Minnie and Maggie were in the kitchen, Minnie cavorting in circles around Maggie's feet while Maggie picked up what looked like the entire contents of the kitchen tidy from the floor.

'Problem?' he asked, and Maggie looked up and grimaced at him.

'She may have been fed but Minnie obviously felt food wasn't enough and showed her disapproval of our late arrival home by strewing the contents of the kitchen tidy across the floor.'

She dumped the last piece of rubbish into a plastic garbage bag, tied the top of it and washed her hands.

'Let's hope it's not a new habit she's developed,' Phil said, then added, 'What a bad dog!' to Minnie who was now leaping around his feet.

'I'll put the bin on the table tomorrow morning just in case,' Maggie told him, and smiled as he continued to tell off the dog.

'I don't think she understands the concept of ''bad dog'',' she said. 'I tried to point out the error of her ways and she seemed to think she'd been extraordinarily clever to have spread it all so far.'

'Do you want me to run a mop over the floor before I go?' Phil asked, and Maggie laughed.

'To prove how domesticated you are? No way—you get back up to the hospital to Pete, I'll mop.'

She smiled at him, and Phil saw the teasing laughter in her face and read it in her night-dark eyes.

'OK?' she said. Just one word. But again Phil felt that little hitch in the region of his heart and wondered what was happening to him.

Could he be falling in love with Maggie? he wondered as he walked back to the hospital.

Now, that *would* be a disaster! He didn't need a psychiatrist or psychoanalyst to tell him that. He wasn't in the first flush of youth and knew all about genetics, so he was reasonably sure he'd inherited enough of his father's genes to make him a poor prospect in the love stakes. It wasn't that he deliberately set out to hurt the women he fell in love with, it was just that, for him, love didn't seem to last and, having lived with pretence in his parents' marriage, he knew he couldn't live a lie himself.

So he'd always been honest. He'd told the women—there had only been three, not three dozen—that he no longer loved them, and had seen their hurt first-hand. Since the third of them he no longer dated seriously—just going out a few times with women who knew that was all a relationship with him would be. Something pleasurable, he hoped, but casual.

But Maggie was different. There was nothing casual about either the hospital Maggie or the dancing Maggie. Both lived their lives with intensity and passion, though the hospital Maggie kept these emotions under tighter control.

'So, Minnie Min, what do I do about that man?' Maggie asked when she'd finished mopping the kitchen floor and had decided to forgive the mischievous dog.

'It's the baby,' Maggie explained because the dog was the most receptive audience she knew and wouldn't pass on any secrets. 'I know I should tell him, and I will—if I manage to hang on to it—but when I do that, is he likely to go all Sir Galahad about it and insist on marriage?'

The thought of marrying Phil sent a shiver of delicious delight through her body, but a loveless marriage would be infinitely worse than no marriage at all, and she would hate to see Phil tied up that way because it would mean he'd be living out his worst nightmare—a replica of his parents' marriage.

'I'll just wait and see,' she finally decided, sharing this with Minnie in case the dog was worrying. 'If I do go past three months, it will still be wintry and I can bundle up in warm clothes and no one will notice for a while—though I guess even without warm clothes no one will notice for a while.'

But that thought depressed her immeasurably. Being pregnant was a great and joyous thing—exciting and exhilarating. She should be shouting her news from the rooftops, not moping in the kitchen, sharing the news with a dog, even if the dog in question did have understanding eyes.

She pressed her hand to her stomach and offered a silent apology to the small cluster of cells busy multiplying inside her.

'I'll tell my mother when I get to three months,' she promised them. 'She'll be excited with me.'

For a moment or two, Maggie amended in her head, *until she asks me who the father is and when we're getting married.*

But if all went well and she had the baby, her family would stand by her, so Baby Walsh would have heaps of cuddles and grow up wrapped in family love.

'But we're getting way too far ahead of ourselves,' she said, ruffling the curls on the top of Minnie's head. She lifted the little dog and put her in her basket, then turned out the kitchen light and made her way upstairs.

Passing Phil's room, even knowing he wasn't in it,

she couldn't help but feel a twinge of regret. Here they were, two adults, who'd already enjoyed a night of explosive and satisfying love-making and could, as they were living in the same house, continue to enjoy such nights, yet they were sleeping in their own rooms— alone in their big beds.

But in her heart she knew that spending even one more night in Phil's arms, in either of their beds, would only deepen what she felt for him, which would undoubtedly lead to her being tempted if the time came that he asked her to marry him. And there they'd be, she head over heels in love with a husband to whom the concept of love was foreign.

Although if I did the stay-at-home-wife thing and provided him with all the love he needs, surely that might work, a sneaky inner voice said temptingly, but Maggie knew it wouldn't. She'd feel cheated and become frustrated, and what kind of mother would she then be for her baby?

'You're a problem,' she said, patting her stomach, but she said it with love because she couldn't help the excitement building inside her, even if she wasn't shouting it from the rooftops.

Yet!

CHAPTER SIX

THE solution to one of her problems, when to tell Phil she was pregnant, came much sooner than Maggie had anticipated. Not because morning sickness struck with such intensity she couldn't hide the fact but because of one small dog who had suddenly decided she didn't like being left alone in the house.

True, Mayarma, the dog walker, called for Minnie every day and took her for a long walk and play in the park, but Minnie still felt obliged to show her dissatisfaction with her lack of company by strewing rubbish across the floor. Remembering to put the kitchen tidy on the bench became as high a priority as locking the front door, but as Minnie rarely ventured upstairs, Maggie hadn't given a thought to the small waste-paper basket in her *en suite* bathroom.

'Not again,' Phil groaned as they came home together one evening and opened the door to see a trail of rubbish leading down the stairs. 'My turn to do the clean-up,' he said. He lifted the milk they'd bought on the way home out of the plastic bag, passed the bottle to Maggie and kept the bag for the rubbish.

Maggie, admonishing the little dog all the way, went on through to the kitchen to put the milk in the fridge.

With the door still open she pulled out some chicken breasts and an assortment of vegetables. She'd make a stir-fry and rice—easy meal to prepare yet filling enough to satisfy Phil's appetite. Her own appetite was on the wane at the moment, and though she wasn't

83

feeling nauseous at any stage of the day she also wasn't hungry.

She was slicing celery into long julienne strips and pushing them across to sit beside the similarly sliced capsicum on the cutting board, idly admiring the contrasting colours, when she heard Phil come down the stairs, across the polished wooden floor of the living room and into the kitchen.

Would she always be as conscious of his footsteps?

Would her heartbeat continue to accelerate as he got closer, so whenever she was in his presence there was turmoil in her chest?

Should she leave work now—return to Melbourne—before this whole 'love for Phil' condition got totally out of hand?

He didn't say anything and she kept chopping, assuming he was getting a light beer out of the fridge, but she didn't hear the fridge door. In fact, she heard a chair scrape across the tiles and guessed he'd just sat down.

Determined not to give in to the urge to turn and look at him—looking at him at home was so different to looking at him at work—she pulled a head of broccoli towards her and began to separate it into small flowerets.

'Stir-fry and rice OK with you?' she asked, when the silence became too much to bear.

'Fine,' he said.

Hard to read much into a single word.

Was he reading something that he hadn't said more? Hadn't started some general conversation about work or housekeeping, the two subjects they both seemed to feel were safe?

Maggie began to slice the beans.

'Alex and Annie are due back Saturday.' Great—tell the man something he already knows, why don't you? 'I wondered if we should have them down for dinner Saturday night. And Rod, of course. And Henry if he's well enough to have Minnie clambering all over him. I thought I could do a Japanese meal. Is Alex into raw fish and seaweed and things like that?'

When silence greeted this offering Maggie realised there was something going on behind her back she didn't know about. Something she guessed she didn't want to know about!

She stopped cutting, terrified her suddenly trembling hands would send the knife slicing through her fingers if she continued.

Then she turned around to see Phil sitting exactly where she'd envisaged him at the table. On the table, on a tissue, directly in front of him, was the test strip from the second pregnancy kit, with its telltale stripe across it.

'I realise it's none of my business, and a gentleman should simply have dropped it into the bag with the rest of the rubbish. But then I thought about repercussions, your work as part of Alex's team, and also how you might be feeling yourself—up here without your family and as far as I know no man in your life to support you—so I thought maybe it would be best to talk to you about it.'

His eyes, expressionless, were fixed on Maggie's face as he said these things, and as she could feel her blood pounding through her veins, she guessed her cheeks were, by now, a bright, rosy red.

She opened her mouth to say something—anything, yell at him perhaps for not minding his own business—but no words came out.

'I won't hassle you, Mags,' he said gently, 'but I do want you to know that I'm here for you. I'll help you any way I can, listen if you need to talk things through, make cups of tea for you in the morning if you're sick—be there for you.'

He paused to smile at her, but it was the saddest smile Maggie had ever seen and its sadness pierced her heart.

'After all, isn't that what being housemates is all about?'

It was at this stage Maggie realised there was something wrong with the conversation.

Oh, she was hearing it all right, it just wasn't coming through in her head as clearly as it might be. Like trying to see through thick fog and catching only blurry outlines, what she was hearing was distorted in some way.

'Have you told the guy?'

The fog lifted—though in her head, not his. He certainly hadn't the foggiest notion that the baby might be his.

And why should he? They'd used protection, but somehow something had happened and it hadn't been enough...

Phil thought he'd got through the conversation remarkably well. His first instinct on seeing the test strip had been disbelief. How could Maggie have made love to him when she was seeing someone else?

Pain—jealous pain—that she *was* seeing someone else intervened!

Then anger had begun to smoulder—not at Maggie but at the someone else. Where was the blighter? He certainly wasn't around at the moment because Phil knew Maggie, apart from an occasional night out at a club, was, at the moment, leading as non-existent a social life as he did.

Was the father someone she'd been seeing in Melbourne?

Dancing with?

Questions bombarded him, which was just as well as they stopped him thinking about the nauseous feeling creeping over him, as if Maggie's pregnancy was a personal disappointment.

Anyway, he'd got this far, made his stand—he'd look after her, that was what he was saying—but she obviously hadn't caught onto the gist of it for she was still staring at the strip on the table in front of him with a kind of mesmerised horror.

Pity for her pushed him to his feet, and he walked around the table, put his arm around her and led her to a chair.

'I'm sorry if you'd have preferred I didn't say anything, but I wanted you to know I'm on your side—that you're not alone in this.'

He pressed a kiss to the top of her head, and thought ugly thoughts about the man who'd abandoned her. And abandoned she must have been to be keeping the pregnancy a secret.

Although maybe she'd only just found out.

Or maybe she hadn't kept it a secret. Maybe she'd told a lot of people, just not him.

Now disappointment surged through the turmoil of emotions he was suffering.

She pushed away from him and sank down into the chair he'd pulled out for her, then rested her elbows on the table and pressed her head into her hands, so all he could see was the pale nape of her neck where her dark hair parted and fell to each side.

Inappropriate thoughts about kissing that pale sliver

of skin formed in his head, but he held them at bay with practicality.

'Is there something I can get you? A coffee—no, best you don't have coffee! How early in pregnancy do you have to give up coffee? Do you know? I'll look it up for you. That'll probably be the hardest part for a caffeine addict like you. I'll make a cup of tea.'

Pleased to have something to do, he crossed to the bench, filled the kettle and turned it on. Seeing beans half-sliced, he finished them while the kettle boiled then made two mugs of tea and carried them across to the table, tea bag strings still dangling over the sides.

'I've never made tea for you before so don't know how you take it,' he said to the still bent head. 'Black, two sugars, like you do coffee?'

He was being so helpful Maggie knew she had to respond. But how? By telling him she hated tea and would sooner drink poison?

Talk about biting the hand that fed you!

'What you could do is get rid of that test strip,' she managed to say, her voice croaking out from somewhere near her boots.

'Oh, dear,' she heard Phil say as he bundled the offending article back into its tissue and dropped it in the kitchen bin. 'Do I take it you're not happy about this pregnancy? Are you thinking about a termination?'

Maggie sighed and lifted her head.

'How could I possibly be happy about it?' she demanded, knowing her words and her tone were too sharp when concern registered in his eyes. 'The six months I worked with you and Alex in Melbourne were great, but to be offered the opportunity to do another twelve months with him was better, in my opinion, than winning Lotto! With his name on my CV my dream of getting a fellowship at a hospital in the US might just have come true! Now this!'

He sat down opposite her and jiggled his tea bag in his tea.

'So, you're thinking termination?'

His voice was so full of sympathetic understanding she wanted to slap him, but she didn't, making do with a good yell instead.

'No, I'm not thinking termination!' she roared, frightening Minnie out of the room. The sight of the little dog scuttling to safety calmed her down somewhat and she added in a more reasonable voice, 'I'm sorry. This is bad timing but nothing more than that. I've only known a week—that test was the second one—and I need time to get used to the idea myself. And it's early days yet—think of the statistics, I may not hold onto it—but termination?'

Her anger died away completely and she shuddered, then hid it with a weak smile.

'It fits with some people's lives and at another time, under other circumstances, I might have considered it. But I've seen too many babies die, Phil—babies I've not been able to save, so, no, this baby is mine and if I can carry it safely through to term, I'm keeping it.'

She realised as she finished the sentence just how fiercely protective she'd sounded, and found that one hand had yet again crept to curl above her stomach.

Ridiculous when the embryo was still not much more than a heart in a curl of developing cells.

Even more ridiculous to get attached when she'd twice miscarried…

*   *   *

She must love the father, to be so definite about it. Maybe he's married. Bet if he is she doesn't tell him, she's so damn independent.

Phil realised he was still jiggling his tea bag and looked down to see the liquid had turned a tarry black. He didn't like tea much at the best of times, but this would be impossible to drink.

Maggie didn't seem too keen on hers either. She was turning the mug in circles the way his nanny had done with the teapot as she'd waited for the leaves to settle.

Had the old woman returned to earth to haunt him that he was thinking about her so often these days?

No, it was Maggie's fault—with all her poking and probing about his home life.

He looked up from the tarry tea to see her watching him—Maggie, not his nanny's ghost.

Consideringly…

'I've never seen you drink tea,' she said, just when he thought their conversation might become deep and meaningful.

'I hate it,' he admitted, and she laughed and pushed her mug across the table to him.

'Me, too,' she said, 'though maybe I'd better get used to it. Or start drinking decaffeinated coffee!' She shuddered. 'Doesn't bear thinking about, does it? And as for the headaches! Believe me, I've tried to give up coffee before and the caffeine-withdrawal headaches are sheer murder. Days and days of them. And I won't be able to take anything to relieve them, so be prepared for a very cranky colleague.'

She pushed the chair back as if the conversation was now finished, picked up both mugs of tea and carried them over to the sink, where she emptied them out.

Then she returned to her cutting and slicing, throw-

ing only the most casual of remarks over her shoulder.
'You didn't say if chicken stir-fry is OK with you?'

So much for sharing with your housemate!

So much for his offer of support!

'Yes, thanks,' he said, glaring at Minnie who'd come
back in from the garden and was looking for some
attention. Then he left the room, going not upstairs but
to the downstairs room Alex had set up as a library.
He'd look up some medical books and find out just
when things like the mother's caffeine intake became
unsafe to a foetus.

Whether Maggie liked it or not, he was going to be
with her every step of the way through this pregnancy.

In fact, he was quite looking forward to it. A kind
of surrogate fatherhood.

As he pulled down a tome on obstetrics he found
himself hoping she wouldn't give up her job too
soon—wouldn't move back to Melbourne to have the
baby.

Though it was strange to be feeling so proprietorial
an interest in it!

Maggie finished chopping the vegetables, sliced two
chicken breasts and turned on the heat under the wok.
She was concentrating so fiercely on what she was doing—to prevent thinking about the repercussions of
Phil's discovery—she didn't notice her pager buzzing
on the kitchen table.

'Hospital. A two-week-old being transferred from up
the coast—aortic stenosis, picked up late, already
treated with a balloon catheterisation that has failed.'

Maggie turned off the gas, tipped her sliced vegetables onto one plate, the chicken onto another, covered
both with clingwrap and washed her hands. Personal

problems were forgotten as she translated Phil's words into a rehearsal of what lay ahead of them.

For a start, the baby would require the operation Phil had refused to do the previous week, but this time there was no alternative. It was too late for prostaglandin to keep the ductus arteriosis open because the little duct would already have closed and be disintegrating, as it was supposed to do once a baby started breathing air. But a tiny balloon, inserted through a catheter and inflated to force the aortic valves open, had failed to do its job, and Phil would now have to operate to open them or refashion them into working entities.

'Rachel and Kurt on their way?' she asked, pausing in the hall to get her jacket. Phil already had it, and held it out for her to put on. She thought of the hug he'd given her last time he'd helped her into it, and knew this time he was the one who needed the hug.

But he was all business, and she knew he wouldn't appreciate the hug—probably wouldn't even know what it was for!

They walked briskly up to the hospital, at first in silence, each thinking of the tasks that lay ahead, then Phil said, 'Alex is so much better at talking to parents than I am.'

Maggie turned to look at him and saw a deep frown scoring his forehead.

'I wouldn't have thought so. The times I've heard Alex talk, I've wondered why the parents have gone ahead with the op.'

Phil's frown cleared as he offered her a brief smile.

'That's exactly what I mean. He's able to tell them the downside of things so matter-of-factly they accept it, while I hate having to say, ''There's a thirty per cent chance your baby won't come out of this alive.'' I *hate* having to tell people that, Mags.'

Unable to think of any comfort she could offer, Maggie took his hand and squeezed it, and they walked the rest of the way hand in hand.

Within fifteen minutes of the page they were talking to the parents, Maggie anxious to find out about previous procedures the baby had had and what reaction, if any, little Cain had had to anaesthetic.

Maria Cardella, Cain's mother, was sitting by the bed where her little son lay, hooked up to a ventilator and monitor, while Al, the father, paced the room.

'All operations, particularly on infants this young, carry an element of risk. In this case, we will be opening up Cain's chest, cutting through tissue to get to his heart and putting him onto a bypass machine that will put oxygen into his blood and keep blood flowing around his body. The machine has refrigeration that will cool the blood and cool Cain, so eventually we can turn off the machine for a short time to work inside his heart and fix the valve. By cooling him we reduce the demand for blood from other organs in the body.'

Maggie watched the faces of the two parents. They looked as if they were desperately trying to understand what Phil was telling them, but a glazed look in their eyes suggested it was too much information.

Yet they had to know.

'The way valves work is they open up as the heart pumps blood into the arteries, then close so it can't rush back into the ventricles. Because the base of the artery we're concerned with, the aorta, is inside the heart, we have to go in there to fix the valves. Once in his heart, we'll see just how bad his valves are. Hopefully, we can open them up by trimming them a bit, and they'll keep working just fine.'

Or Cain might need new valves grafted in, which would mean more operations as he grew to replace them when they became too small and started to leak.

Maggie, reading carefully through Cain's case notes, thought this but didn't say it. It was hard enough for parents to comprehend that their beautiful new baby had life-threatening problems, then to have to take in what the surgeons were going to do to him and understand enough to give informed consent to the procedure, without complications way down the track being pointed out.

Phil was answering Al's questions now, while Maria sat beside her infant son, fat tears sliding down her cheeks.

'We want you to do whatever you can, and if it doesn't work for him, that's how it has to be,' Al said at last, and Maggie wondered how he would feel when asked to sign the consent form, something a nurse would ask of him as little Cain was being wheeled into Theatre.

'Have you got all you need?' Phil asked, and Maggie, realising he was talking to her, nodded, but stayed in the room and spoke quietly to Maria.

'We'll take real good care of him,' she said, and the woman looked up and nodded, accepting Maggie's word that everything that could possibly be done for her baby would be done.

'I hate it when it's their first baby,' Rachel said, coming into Theatre while Maggie was checking she had all she'd need. 'I mean, they're so excited, first baby and all, then, whammo, some person they don't know is telling them there are terrible things wrong with their new son. *Terrible* things.'

Maggie looked at the theatre sister and saw the despair she'd heard in Rachel's voice mirrored on her face. In the nearly eight months she'd worked with Rachel, Maggie had never heard her upset—or even slightly downbeat.

'Are you OK?' she asked.

'There is no OK!' Rachel said, echoing something surgeons often said in Theatre. In top surgeons' eyes OK was just not good enough. Perfect was their aim and that's how they wanted things to be.

'There is for ordinary humans like you and me,' Maggie reminded her. 'Sometimes OK is as good as you can expect, although there's always hope we'll better it.'

Rachel smiled at her.

'I'm grumpy, that's all. I've been doing this work for eight years and I love it. I'm good at it. I can see things Alex and Phil can't see because they're focussed on what they're doing, and I can react to things when I see them because I've seen enough of all the ops they do to know how it should go, and now I hear the fellow who operated last week—when Phil wouldn't—is telling people things went wrong because of inadequate theatre staff.'

'He what?' Maggie couldn't believe it. 'But he's at Children's—how come the stories are circulating here?'

'By kind favour of the great Dr Ellis, of course,' Rachel snapped.

'And no Annie here to put out the fire,' Maggie muttered, thinking of the damage this could do the fledgling unit. 'But don't take it all personally, Rachel. I'm theatre staff too, I'm sure he's blaming all of us equally. What about Scott?'

'What about Scott?' that man said, coming into Theatre, a bright scarf wrapped around his head and his gown on, but not yet gloved.

'Dr Ellis's rumours,' Rachel said succinctly.

'Oh, that!' Scott said, his usual good cheer dissipating immediately. 'It shouldn't worry you, you work for Alex. What about me? These last two months have been like a revelation. I mean, I liked hearts and had decided cardiac surgery was definitely for me, but this stuff? Watching Alex and Phil work? It's so beautiful. I know for certain now that it's what I want to do, but if I end up carrying the can for that operation, who knows where I'd get another position in paeds cardiac surgery?'

'Damn Ellis!' Maggie said, but inside she felt a growing concern. Paediatric heart surgery required one hundred per cent concentration from everyone in the team, yet here were two members, three counting her, four counting Phil, who were already uptight before the operation began.

'Forget it all,' Kurt said, and Maggie realised she hadn't known he was there. Well, she probably *had* known, but he said so little from behind his machine they tended to take him as another piece of furniture. 'We've got this baby coming in. That's all we need to think about now. Later we'll talk about these rumours and work out a strategy for dealing with them, but the little fellow we're operating on today needs and deserves all of our attention.'

It was the most Maggie had ever heard Kurt say, and

she was impressed. She told him so, then left Theatre, wanting to supervise the transfer of Cain from his room herself.

Scott opened Cain's chest, Rachel sliding the stainless-steel clamps into place and cranking open the rib cage so Scott could go further, cauterising small vessels as he went. He cut open the pericardium, the tough fibrous sac around the heart, and put in a stitch to hold it to the chest wall so Phil would have a clear field around the heart.

Maggie watched her monitors, tensely alert for any change in the baby's status.

She felt rather than heard Phil come into Theatre, then his quiet 'Good job' to Scott confirmed his presence. She glanced his way. With mask and loupe and light all strapped around his head, it was hard to see skin let alone read expression, but listening to his voice, seeing the sure way his hands moved, she doubted he'd heard the rumours.

She prayed he hadn't, because the slightest lapse in concentration could lead to disaster.

Not that there wasn't a little of that. Phil's soft comment 'I've never seen a malformation like this!' was the first indication something was wrong.

'That's the left coronary artery,' he said to Scott and the other registrar assisting, 'and instead of curving around the heart to feed the left atrium and ventricle, it's shunted a large part of itself off into the inferior vena cava. I've read about it but never seen it.'

Without wasting more than a fleeting second wishing Alex was around, Phil began the process of attaching Cain to the bypass machine, first inserting cannulae to take the plastic tube to and from the machine.

Maggie administered the drugs to keep the baby's

blood from clotting and clogging up the machine, and more drugs that prevented the fragile blood cells being damaged, then Cain was on bypass and Phil could tackle the problem of the displaced coronary artery first.

'You have to wonder if lack of blood to the left ventricle has been preventing it pumping effectively enough to push blood into the aorta. Is it possible the valves are OK? Why wasn't this picked up? I wonder if anyone did an oesophageal echo to get a better view. Maggie, did you see one?'

'Not in the notes I read,' Maggie told him, but they all knew notes that followed a baby from one hospital to another were sometimes not complete.

'I guess they put it down to a left ventricle insufficiency—maybe a hypoblast, which is common with aortic stenosis,' Phil continued, almost speaking to himself, so Maggie wondered if he was just thinking it through out loud.

'Whatever they put it down to, it's our problem now, isn't it?' Scott said, and Maggie turned in time to see Phil nod.

She could almost feel his concentration. The problem with moving coronary arteries was that they could kink easily, and once kinked would starve the heart muscles of the blood they needed to keep pumping.

'We can take a vein from his chest if we need to, and use it to repair the artery or replace it,' Phil said as he worked, and Maggie had to admire the fact that he kept explaining what he was doing to Scott and the other registrar even when things were tough.

'Done! Now for the little fellow's heart.'

The bypass machine was turned off to stop it sucking in air when the heart stopped beating, then an injection was given into the coronary arteries to stop the heart. Now Phil worked swiftly, making an incision high up on the left ventricle to reach the opening of the aorta.

Maggie watched her monitors, checked everything was in place for an emergency and did her own monitoring of the tension levels in the room.

Not too tight, she decided, and the quiet buzz of orders suggested nothing major was going wrong.

So far so good!

'Now, make sure you suction all the air out of his heart before we put him back on bypass. We get air into the machine, we put it back into his blood and the poor kid has a stroke.'

Phil the teacher telling Scott what to watch for! He did it well, Maggie realised, and more consistently than Alex did, though both of them, when concentrating on the intricacy of the surgery they performed, would sometimes forget to explain.

'Pump back on,' Phil said to Kurt, when they were satisfied the tiny heart was airtight.

The noise of the pump, this time pumping warmed blood into Cain's body, thumped through the room, a background noise to Phil's quiet voice, telling Scott where he wanted drains and wires and catheters placed.

'OK!' One word, but it signalled it was time to breathe easily again. Maggie saw Phil step back so Scott could close.

Now Maggie, monitoring the atmosphere, could sense a general relaxation in the room.

'He's all yours, Maggie,' Scott said at last, and the surgical staff drifted from the room, leaving the theatre orderly and a junior theatre nurse to clean up the mess they'd left behind.

Rather than shift infants from Theatre to a recovery

room then into the ICU, Maggie kept them in Theatre until she felt it was safe to move them. With little Cain she wanted to wait until she was sure even something as unthreatening as changing his ventilation from the theatre lines to bagging him on the short journey wouldn't compromise his condition.

Twenty minutes later, she was sure he could make the trip safely and called up an ICU nurse and orderly to move him with her. And though the nurse would usually handle the bagging, squeezing air into his ventilator tube using a rubber device they called a bag, Maggie did it herself.

For some reason—and she suspected it had more to do with Phil than being pregnant—she wanted everything to go just right for Cain.

Once in his room she hooked him up to the ventilator again, while the nurse made sure the monitor leads weren't tangled and connected the monitor to the central nursing station.

His parents came in, peering anxiously at the still unconscious baby, and while Maria took the chair beside his bed Al paced.

'The doctor said it went well. He said there could be complications but so far everything's looking good. Is that right?'

Maggie knew she needed confirmation of what Phil had already told her, so she repeated the reassurances, but explained they still had a way to go.

'We'll keep him in here while he's on the ventilator,' she explained, 'but once he comes off that and is breathing on his own, he'll go into the infants' ward where nursing staff especially trained to deal with post-operative cardiac patients will look after him.'

Maria smiled at her.

'Every stage is a little step towards his being better, isn't it?' she said, and Maggie had to agree with her.

Very small steps babies made at times, but each one significant in its own way. It was good for a parent to understand this and take joy in each stage of the recovery.

Maggie left the room, though she knew she'd be back before she left the hospital, checking on how the baby was doing on the ventilator and if there was any sign of distress showing up. But right now the parents needed to be alone with their child and she needed a coffee.

Back in their rooms, the coffee-machine was on but the place was deserted.

'Just how badly are you going to be affected by caffeine?' she asked the embryo developing inside her, then she sighed and drank some water, just in case the word she hadn't heard had been 'badly'!

'Look, decaffeinated coffee-grounds.'

Phil swept into the rooms, waving the packet in the air.

'I knew the canteen served it, so I went down and begged to be allowed to buy some.'

Maggie hid the start of joy his sudden appearance had caused. Hid it with cross words!

'You put that stuff into the machine and you'll be lynched,' she told him.

'No one will know!' he said, still beaming with his cleverness. 'We tip it into the other packet and how would anyone tell? We all drink far too much coffee and we know caffeine's no good for us, so we're really doing the whole team a favour.'

Maggie looked at him, propped herself against a desk and shook her head.

'Phil, you can't do this! Of course people will know. Have you ever drunk decaffeinated coffee? It tastes like—well, it tastes terrible. And people will say so and Becky will get the blame for buying cheap grounds and they'll throw out that lot and buy new, and you can't keep replacing it with decaff!'

He was still holding the packet, but now looked so downcast she had to laugh.

'It's OK—we'll take it home and I'll drink it there.'

'And say what when the others ask what's happened to your eight cups a day coffee habit?'

'I'll tell them I've given up for Lent—no, it's too late for Lent. I'll say I'm doing it for a bet. You bet me I couldn't. They know we're living together, so they'll think it's something that's arisen from that.'

'Living together!' Phil echoed, then he added in a very quiet voice, 'It has other connotations, doesn't it, Mags?'

CHAPTER SEVEN

MAGGIE got up from the desk and poured herself another glass of cold water from the jug in the small fridge.

'Of course it does,' she said, hoping the word 'bracing' might describe her tone but doubting it. Phil's question had gone directly to her heart, piercing the feeble defences she'd been building up around it. 'That's happened with so many words these days. Take "partner", for example. My sister is married, and she's also a partner in a decorating firm, but when I talk about her partner, people assume I mean the man she's living with, who is, in fact, her husband—'

'We weren't talking about words,' Phil interrupted, crossing to where Maggie stood by the fridge, sipping at the cold water, which was having no effect whatsoever on either her nerves or her caffeine craving.

He took the water glass out of her hand and set it down on a table.

'We're talking about living together.'

He put his hands on her shoulders, resting them there, not holding her, but she knew if she moved the pressure might increase.

'Is the father of this baby someone who's important in your life, Maggie? Is he still around? Will he take on the responsibility of a child? Does he want to marry you? Do you want to marry him?'

Yes, yes, I don't know, I don't know and...

If he'd stopped after any of the earlier questions,

Maggie wouldn't have known what to answer, because she hadn't yet thought through all the consequences of telling Phil the baby was his. But the last question was easy to answer.

'No,' she said. 'I don't want to marry him.'

No need to explain she couldn't bear the thought of forcing him into marriage—all she had to do was answer the question.

'You could marry me,' Phil said, and Maggie felt her knees give way, and was sure she would have dropped to the floor if Phil hadn't grabbed her.

'Damn,' he said. 'You haven't eaten and I'm keeping you here, talking.'

He sat her down and rummaged in the cupboard, coming back with a packet of biscuits.

'Eat a few of these then I'll take you down to the canteen for dinner. You've got to start thinking about regular meals, Mags,' he said, opening the fridge and taking out the milk.

He sniffed at it and shook his head, then, still holding the milk carton, he fixed his blue eyes on her and added, 'And I meant what I said about marrying you. Think about it. We're already living together, so the logistics would be simple. We work together, so we understand the stresses of each other's job—none better. The baby will have a hands-on father, and we were great together in bed.'

Maggie felt the air around her grow suddenly colder, then heard Phil repeat the words in a slow, hoarse voice.

'We were great together in bed!'

He stared at Maggie, disbelief and anger vying for control of his features.

Anger won.

'Is it my baby, Maggie?' he asked, his voice soft but no less furious for its softness. 'It is, isn't it? And just when were you going to share this little gem of knowledge with me? Just how long did you intend letting me believe it was someone else's?'

Maggie felt the icy wind of his fury and though she wasn't nearly ready for him to have found out, she found some relief in his anger because it fired hers up as well.

'For heaven's sake, Phil, I've only just found out myself. I'm still trying to come to terms with the fact that a one-night stand with a colleague has ended in a pregnancy! How do you think *I* feel? And what would you suggest I do? Front up one day in the PICU and say, "Oh, by the way, I'm pregnant and it's yours!" Hell, Phil, I know the kind of childhood you had, I know you have your own dreams of the way a marriage should work, and I also know that with the stupid male chivalry you carry around, the first thing you'd do when I told you would be to ask me to marry you.'

Maggie gave a mirthless laugh then added, 'You did that anyway—even thinking it was someone else's baby—so I was spot on, wasn't I?'

'This isn't about my offer of marriage—it's about you not telling me the baby is mine. It's about being a biological cipher all over again—an accident of paternity. Well, that's not going to happen.'

Maggie could feel his anger vibrating around the room, but she couldn't find words to deflect or defuse it, so she sat and let it wash around her.

'My child is going to know his father and know his father's love.'

It's about the baby, Maggie thought sadly. Only about the baby!

Phil finished speaking then heard the silence echoing back to him and realised he'd been shouting.

He glanced at Maggie, saw the way her hand curved protectively across her stomach and felt a momentary pang of compunction.

But she *was* wrong, not telling him.

She was also awfully pale and he remembered how she'd come close to fainting earlier.

'Come on,' he said, taking her by the arm and hauling her out of the chair. 'You need to eat and this is hardly the time or place to be discussing the matter.'

He knew he'd spoken brusquely, but her pale face and the lines of strain at the corners of her mouth had made him feel angry again—and protective—and...

Husbandly?

He had no idea how that would feel, but as he hustled Maggie towards the lift, he decided he'd better find out—and soon. There was no way a child of his would be born out of wedlock.

Was that a hopelessly old-fashioned attitude?

A relic of his upbringing?

Best not to say it to Maggie!

But there was no reason why he and Maggie couldn't make a go of marriage.

He must have spoken this thought out loud, because Maggie's 'Oh, please, Phil!' had to be in response to it.

Though when she added, 'I need food but not so badly I have to run all the way to the canteen,' he wondered if he *had* said it. Maybe she'd been protesting the pace.

Which meant he'd have to say it again!

He slowed down but kept his grip on her arm, telling himself it was a supporting grip not a proprietorial one, though something very like a proprietorial feeling, where Maggie was concerned, was creeping over him.

Would it take over from the 'race her off to bed' feeling he usually had to deal with whenever he was around her?

They had just reached the canteen when both their pagers went off.

'You stay here and eat,' Phil ordered, directing Maggie towards the food counter in the nearly deserted canteen. 'I'll check out what's wrong.'

'Nonsense. It's the PICU so it's sure to be Cain. I'm going straight up there.'

Don't let him die! Maggie found herself praying as they both hurried back to the lift, then felt a moment of shame because she was wishing this for Phil's sake, not the baby's.

But it wasn't Cain who was the problem, but little Amy Carter, who'd received the new heart two months earlier.

'High temp, evidence of infection. I didn't know if you'd have to take her into Theatre so I called both of you,' the sister in charge of the PICU told them. 'I've paged the rest of the team and will ask them to be on standby just in case, but I knew you two would still be in the hospital.'

The little girl had been hooked up to the ventilator and monitors by the intensivist who'd admitted her to the unit. She was obviously very ill, and her mother was shaking with anxiety.

Phil spoke gently to the little girl as he examined her, while Maggie led Mrs Carter to a chair and sat her down.

'She's been through so much,' Mrs Carter cried. 'First, being so sick, she needed the operation and then after it—you remember how everything went wrong for her. Then just as she's getting better, this!'

'Has she been with any other children who might have been in contact with chickenpox?' Phil asked, and Maggie wondered if he'd gone mad. What did chicken-pox have to do with anything? The little girl was a heart transplant patient!

'Her cousins have all got it, but I keep Amy away from other children—I mean, she's not long out of hos-pital and Dr Attwood warned me about infection. I keep her in her own room whenever anyone is visiting.'

But family members would want to see her, Maggie thought, especially inquisitive children.

'She's got chickenpox?' she asked aloud, and Phil nodded.

'I think so. Poor pet! With the scar on her chest still healing, it's hard to tell if the small marks there are the beginning of chickenpox lesions, but I'd say they are. The blood tests should be back soon.'

'Chickenpox! It's only chickenpox!' Mrs Carter said, her voice so full of relief and joy Maggie didn't want to tell her the bad news.

But Phil would have to!

'I'm afraid it's not all that much of a relief,' he said gently, coming to rest against the bed in front of the sitting woman. 'Because Amy is on so many anti-rejection drugs, and these drugs are designed to damp down the body's immune system, a virus like this can take a terrible hold. I'd be lying to you if I didn't tell you we're in for a bad few days. But I'll be here with her all the time, and the staff are trained to be vigilant and know how to keep her as comfortable as possible.'

He took Mrs Carter's hands and continued, 'We haven't got her all this way just to lose her now, so hang in there. It'll be a fight, but it's a fight we can win, so don't give up hope.'

Maggie heard the commitment and determination in his voice and knew what he was thinking—he didn't want Amy Carter crying in his head in the years to come. Her heart ached for him, knowing just how hard he'd take it if he couldn't save Amy, and suddenly she wondered if marrying Phil might not be a good idea. He was deserving of so much love, and she could give it to him. Even if he didn't love her, wouldn't her love help him in some way?

But would he let her love him?

Let her fill some of the empty places in his heart?

She watched him sitting there, talking with Mrs Carter, giving of himself without asking anything in return, then he stood up and left the room, turning back to say to Maggie, 'You should be masked. I'm going to instigate total barrier nursing here, so the infection can't be carried by staff from one room to the next.'

Maggie stayed a little longer then, rather than risk carrying infection into Cain's room, she checked him on the monitors, satisfied herself he was doing well. With exhaustion from the long, long day washing over her, she left the unit and headed home. Forget food, all she wanted was to fall into bed and sleep for ever.

'I don't think I've ever been so pleased to see anyone in my entire life,' she said to Annie and Alex when they, with Annie's dog Henry, appeared at the house late on Saturday afternoon.

Minnie, banned from visiting Henry while he recovered from a series of operations, had gone berserk on seeing her friend, so the two dogs had been banished to the back yard.

Maggie gave both her human visitors a hug and invited them to come through to the kitchen.

'Inviting you into your own house, Alex. That's a bit weird, isn't it?'

'It's your home now—of course you do the inviting. Phil not here?'

'He's at the hospital.'

'Amy Carter?'

Maggie felt instant relief.

'Then he *did* contact you about her,' she said. 'He's so stubborn, I wondered if he would. He kept saying there wasn't anything you could do and you both needed a break and shouldn't be bothered.'

Alex smiled at her while Annie chuckled, and Maggie sensed the love the pair shared and felt a sharp twinge of envy.

'He didn't contact me but I kept in touch with him, not all the time, because the last thing I wanted was for him to think I was checking on him, but just occasionally. Hard to just cut off, you know, and after making excuses to go for a short walk so I could use my mobile, I found Annie had been doing the same, phoning Becky at the unit the moment I went out, just to see how things were going.'

The pair smiled at each other again, their love fairly buzzing in the air around them.

'So you heard about Dr Ellis and his stories.'

As soon as she'd said it she realised they hadn't, for both of them looked puzzled.

'Ellis the cardiologist?' Annie said. 'He doesn't do much work at Jimmie's.'

'Is he the one who wanted Phil to operate on the neonate?' Alex asked, and Maggie nodded, then knew she had to explain. She didn't want either of them walking into what could prove to be a battle, unprepared.

'He's been spreading stories about Phil's refusal to do the op—making out it was incompetence on his part. I know Amy's been terribly sick, and it's been a struggle to get her through this setback, but in some ways it's been good because between her and the scheduled procedures, Phil's been too busy to be worrying about any extraneous matters.'

'Are they affecting the unit?' Annie asked, and Maggie smiled to herself. Just like that, Annie had slipped back into work mode.

'The unit staff are sticking together, confident it was the right decision—but the staff working on the baby ward are finding things tough. I think probably the other staff members were already a little jealous that some staff had been singled out to care for our babies and children, so they've been making snide remarks. But I think the main problem is going to come from the hospital hierarchy.'

'Where there's also been envy of our funding and grumblings about our special treatment all along,' Annie said. 'But it's nothing we can't cope with,' she added determinedly. 'I'd be more worried about how it's affecting Phil.'

Though it wasn't phrased as a question, Maggie knew it was one, and she sighed.

'I honestly don't know,' she admitted. 'He's been all but living at the hospital since Amy was readmitted, and when we do talk it's about work.'

She paused then said to Alex, 'You know him better than the rest of us, but my impression of Phil is that he keeps things bottled up inside him. He's all the bright playboy on the outside—though there's been precious little of that lately—but what's going on in-side is a deep, dark and probably very gloomy mys-tery.'

Annie, perhaps hearing a faint shadow of despair in the words, put her arm around Maggie's shoulders and gave her a hug.

'And I suppose you've just gone on being Maggie, quietly doing your job and keeping everyone focussed on work, no matter what's going on around you.'

'Oh, Phil's done that, too,' Maggie said, trying des-perately to swallow the lump of misery Annie's sym-pathy had brought to her throat. Self-pity, that was all it was. 'And Rachel! Even Kurt's been heard to speak his mind on the subject. All the team have hung tough.'

Alex had moved to the kitchen bench and was filling the kettle with water, and Annie took the opportunity of his distraction to ask another, quieter, question.

'You and Phil?' she whispered, and Maggie shook her head. Annie was the only person she'd told about her night with Phil, and eventually Annie—well, all the team but Annie first—would have to know about her pregnancy.

If it continued past the first trimester...

But right now there was a crisis at the hospital—two crises really, although Amy was certainly getting better so she hardly counted—and that was where everyone's attention should be focussed.

'Black, two sugars?' Alex said, turning from the bench with the jar of coffee in his hand.

'No, tea for me, thanks, Alex,' Maggie told him, then seeing the look of disbelief on both their faces, she told them the story she'd rehearsed on Phil.

'I bet Phil I could give up coffee,' she said, her voice quavering slightly as she remembered the context of that conversation and the delicate stage their discussion had reached when it had all been halted by Amy's return to hospital.

'How do you like your tea, then?' Alex asked, and Maggie smiled at him.

'Black, two sugars, but weak, because to tell you the truth I hate tea. I'd just as soon drink hot water with two sugars, but people would think I was crazy so I wave the tea bag over the top of the cup.'

She was aware Annie was watching her closely and wondered if she could possibly suspect.

From giving up coffee and only drinking very weak tea?

Surely not!

'I was going to have you two and Rod and Henry to dinner tonight to welcome you back, but even if Phil gets away from the hospital he'll probably feel more like sleeping than being polite to guests,' Maggie said, hoping to divert Annie's attention—just in case she was harbouring suspicious thoughts!

'We're tired, too,' Annie said, 'but knowing Alex, he'll be taking Phil's place at the hospital before I've even unpacked our bags.'

She paused then smiled.

'In fact, I might pop up there myself before I unpack. Just so anyone still considering whatever rumours Dr Ellis spread knows I'm around and I intend to fight back.'

Maggie felt a genuine smile spread across her face for the first time, it seemed, in weeks.

'It's good to have you guys back,' she said, and knew they knew she meant it.

They sat down at the table and drank the tea and coffee Alex had made, talking now about the mountains to the west of Sydney and the wonderful time the honeymooners had had exploring them.

'You must go up there while you're in Sydney,' Annie told Maggie. 'It's a really beautiful area.'

'I will,' Maggie promised, thinking a weekend away, on her own, in the mountains, might be the ideal place to think through her future.

Alex and Annie finished their coffee and departed, leaving Henry in the back yard with Minnie because they were heading not back to Annie's house but towards the hospital. Having guessed Alex would stay up there, Maggie wasn't at all surprised to hear Phil's key in the front door only an hour later.

She was in the laundry, doing some hand-washing, and he came through the house to find her there.

'The cavalry arrived just in time,' he said, leaning against the doorjamb and watching her dunk her sweater in soapy water. 'I doubt I'd have lasted another night without a proper sleep.'

Maggie looked at the lines lack of sleep and anxiety had drawn on his face, and her heart ached with a need to hold and comfort him.

Failing that, she could offer practicality.

'Would you like something to eat? I shopped this morning and bought some mini ham and cheese croissants. It would only take a few minutes to heat you a couple, or would you prefer to just fall into bed?'

'Bed, I think,' he said, but he didn't move and the word 'bed' reverberated around the room, heightening Maggie's usual awareness of her colleague and suggesting things it shouldn't.

She squeezed the soapy water out of the sweater and rinsed it under the tap, then emptied the bucket she'd been using and filled it with clean water, conscious all the time of Phil standing there, watching her.

Silence stretched between them—though 'bed' still whispered in her head—and she tried to think just where they'd been in a very awkward conversation earlier in the week before work had driven all personal matters from both their heads.

They hadn't reached any conclusions, she knew that much, and given the sleep deprivation Phil had suffered this week, maybe he'd forgotten the conversation altogether.

Forgotten he'd guessed the one thing she hadn't told him about the baby.

'Sleep deprivation hasn't killed all my brain cells,' he said, as Maggie once again squeezed water—clean this time—from her sweater. 'So, once I've slept we need to talk, Mags.'

She glanced his way and saw he looked even more tired than he had earlier, although earlier she wouldn't have thought it possible. She set the wet sweater down on top of the washing machine and stepped towards him, then put her arms around him and gave him a hug.

'We'll sort it all out,' she promised, though she wasn't sure they could.

But right now this man needed some reassurance before he slept, and how could she deny it to him?

His arms closed around her back and he drew her closer, resting his chin on the top of her head.

'I don't suppose you'd like a snooze yourself,' he asked, his husky voice and awakening body suggesting he wasn't nearly as exhausted as she'd thought.

Before she could think of a casual way to laugh off

the suggestion, he eased her away and used his fore-finger to tilt her chin so he could look into her face.

'I wouldn't do you justice today, but our time will come,' he said, the words a promise she guessed he intended to keep, then he bent and kissed her on the lips and for a few minutes she forgot all the tangled threads that wove around their lives and gave in to the seduction of that embrace.

CHAPTER EIGHT

MAGGIE woke early, and though she felt lethargic and was tempted to have a lazy morning in bed, she knew she needed exercise. She'd get Minnie and go for a walk in the park. No, Minnie had gone to live with Alex at Annie's house where she'd have Henry for canine company and Rod, who lived in the flat downstairs, to see she was fed when all the humans were held up at work.

Well, people could walk in the park without a dog—no rule against that.

Only it didn't appeal.

Maybe she *would* stay in bed.

Not good for the baby, all this lounging around.

OK, I'll walk, she told the nag in her head. *But I'll drive down to the beach and walk there.*

With this decided, she still lingered, reluctant to leave her comfy bed, reliving the magic of the kiss she'd shared with Phil last night. Then a memory of the conversation they'd had before the kiss returned, and she decided she'd be better off being out of the house when he awoke. It was putting off the inevitable, she knew, but she might think more clearly after a brisk walk in the salt air had cleared the cobwebs from her head.

She pulled on a tracksuit and grabbed a jacket, knowing the wind could whip coldly off the sea.

Breakfast first or later? The question was about as much as she could handle this early in the morning, and she'd just decided on later—walk, then breakfast at the beach—when she reached the kitchen and found Phil already there.

'Good morning!' he said, so cheerfully she had to hide a shudder.

'I think that's always a matter of individual opinion,' she muttered at him.

'Not a morning person?' Phil teased. 'Shows how chaotic things have been at work that we've been living together for a fortnight and I didn't know.'

'You didn't need to know,' Maggie told him, then realised she was pursuing the wrong argument. 'Anyway, I am—a morning person, I mean. I like mornings. I'm up and I'm going for a walk. Would someone who wasn't a morning person be doing that?'

Phil looked around and Maggie knew he'd been about to make a smart remark to Minnie, then realised the little dog was no longer there. And the expression of loss on his face made Maggie realise how much Minnie had meant to him—she'd been part of his image of 'home', however temporary that home might have been.

'I'm going down to the beach for a walk—do you want to come?'

It had to be the surge of pity she'd felt that had made her ask. The last person she needed on a head-clearing excursion was Phil.

'Yes, yes I would. Great place to talk about the wedding. I suppose your folks will want you to have a proper one—with you being their daughter and all. Well, your mother probably would want it. Funny how it is with mothers and brides.'

'Phil!'

The name came out louder than Maggie had intended, but at least it stopped him rabbiting on and gave her the opportunity to have her say.

'There is no wedding to discuss. We're not getting married.'

He stared at her in disbelief.

'Of course we're getting married. We're having a baby.'

The look on his face told Maggie he'd realised this wasn't exactly a winning argument, but he recovered, coming towards her and taking hold of her hands.

'I put that badly. The thing is, I've been thinking about it all week and I'd really like to marry you, Mags, baby or not. We'd be good together. We know and understand each other's work and the demands it puts on us. Alex is confident of your work so I'm sure he'd offer you a place on the team in the US. Then when I finish my fellowship with him, we'll still be a team, working together wherever we decide to go.'

It was so exactly the life Maggie had always envisaged—working in partnership with the man she loved, partnership in the ultimate sense, in marriage and in their careers—that she almost weakened and gave in.

But this was her dream, not Phil's, and she doubted it would fill the emptiness in his life.

And what about the emptiness in her own life if she agreed? What about love?

Had she said those three words aloud that Phil's hands tightened on hers?

She must have, because the blue eyes were serious as he said, 'I can't promise that, Mags.'

'So it *is* all about the baby, in spite of what you just said about us being good together.'

He frowned down at her.

'You can't know that and nor do I.'

'Of course I know. Would you have mentioned marriage if I wasn't pregnant?'

'No, but—'

'There are no buts!' Maggie said, and she walked away, knowing the dream on offer wasn't what she wanted after all.

If Phil wanted to walk with her he could follow, but right now, more than ever, she needed that walk. Needed to think.

He did follow, protesting every step of the way, so in the end, as she backed the car out of the garage, she turned to him and said, 'Phil, I'm going for a walk to clear my head and have a think about things. For a start, it's far too early to be thinking in terms of a living, breathing baby.'

Her heart squeezed now with a different pain, remembered pain, and she realised, though she'd intended telling him about her previous miscarriages, she couldn't, fearing it might be an omen of bad luck for this pregnancy.

'Supposing it happens, I understand you want to be involved in the baby's life, and I appreciate that. But it doesn't mean you have to take over *my* life. Anyway, pregnancies last forty weeks—don't you think we've plenty of time to sort out minor details?'

She glanced his way, and saw again the lines of strain on his face, some of them, she knew, caused by her unexpected pregnancy. Then she remembered the stress he'd been under the last few weeks, and regret that she should be providing additional stress made her reach across and touch him lightly on the hand.

'We'll sort it out, but let's think things through first—not rush into the first solution that occurs to us.'

'At least you're saying *us*!' he muttered at her, then

he sighed, rested his head back against the headrest, and closed his eyes.

The parking area at the beach was almost deserted, and Maggie, seeing the wind flapping the crossed red flags that indicated the surf was unsafe for swimmers, wondered if the park might not have been the better option for her walk.

'It's blowing a gale out there,' she said, but Phil was already opening the car door.

'A nice bracing breeze,' he said, grinning at her in a way that started the flip-flops again in her heart. 'Come on!'

He was still too tired to be trying to sort things out between himself and Maggie, Phil had realised as they'd driven towards the beach. Instead of planning a strategy that might work with a fiercely independent woman like Maggie, he'd gone rushing in with his own assumptions and upset her. Now he'd have to go back to square one and start again.

The thought made him feel even more tired, but when they reached the beach and he saw the wind thrashing the tops of the swell to white froth, he felt invigorated, as if this cold, blustery weather would blow all his cares away.

Well, it wouldn't do that, but it would give him an excuse to put his arm around Maggie and maybe give her a warming kind of cuddle. That idea had taken precedence in his mind and all the rest of the stuff there could go hang for a while.

'Come on, you'll be blown away if I don't anchor you to the ground,' he told her, as she tried to escape the first part of his plan.

She turned and smiled at him and, with the wind whipping her dark hair across her face and bringing pinkness to her cheeks, she looked so delectable it was all he could do not to kiss her right there and then.

Caution prevailed, however, and he led her down the concrete steps to the beach, then across the dry sand towards the surf, rolling and crashing onto the shore. It was easier walking on the wet sand and though salt spray caught them occasionally, Maggie didn't seem to mind the dampness that misted in her hair and sparkled like diamonds in the bright morning sunlight.

Diamonds! Would she wear a diamond ring? No, she was a red girl. A ruby? Maybe a square-cut ruby with small diamonds around it. Or a baguette-cut ruby, with baguette diamonds each side. Would she think that too much?

He had no idea, though he did realise that in spite of Maggie's protestation that there'd be no wedding his mind was steadfastly following that track. Of course it would, it was the only sensible solution. In fact, it was such a great solution he felt his body responding every time he thought about it.

He glanced towards her, wondering if the walk was working for her, as far as thinking was concerned. For himself, well, he was thinking, but with her warm, soft body tucked up against his, his thoughts were getting raunchier and raunchier.

'This isn't working,' Maggie said, tugging away from him. 'I can't think with you so close.'

'No?'

Given where his mind had been, it wasn't surprising that hope began to hammer in his heart. Maybe it was hammering harder in other parts of his body, but he was sure it was in his heart as well.

She looked up at him, brown eyes serious, and

though he guessed she'd been feeling some of what he'd been feeling he was sure she was going to lie.

'No!' she snapped crossly. 'All I can think about was how good we were in bed together, and how much I'd like to do it again. I know it's probably just a hormonal thing from the pregnancy, but it's driving me nuts.'

Phil held in his whoop of joy, neither did he scoop her into his arms and run with her all the way back to the car, though both options were distinctly appealing. But he was a mature man of thirty-four, not a randy adolescent, so he made do with pulling her towards him and then kissing her so thoroughly he realised that carrying her off the beach might have been a better way to go. Because now, with the kiss broken off so they could breathe, they still had to get home, and if her legs were anywhere near as shaky as his were, just getting back to the car was going to be an effort.

'You want to do this?' he asked her, as they tumbled into the house, shut the back door and were about to resume kissing.

'So much!' she whispered, her eyes sparkling with desire, her lips so red and ripe his body ached to devour them.

They kissed their way through the kitchen, risked serious injury continuing it up the stairs, then finally he guided her onto his bed, still kissing, but now his hands were exploring her body, and hers his, further inflaming the passionate desire that flared between them.

Maggie could feel heat, but couldn't tell if it was his or hers. The inner heat was hers, but skin heat—that was different. Skin heat brought her nerve endings to life in a way she'd never before experienced, so they zapped and tingled at the slightest touch, the merest brush. She nuzzled her lips against the hot satiny skin of his shoulder and nibbled at his ear-lobe, while his hands explored her belly, fingers tickling at her belly button, sliding lower, her escalating desire causing little whimpering noises of delight and demand to flutter from her lips.

'So sweet,' he whispered, as his lips found hers once again, while his fingers worked a magic of their own. 'Sweet tempestuous delight, Mags, that's what you are.'

Maggie was beyond speech, which was probably just as well, for her words might just have been words of love, confessions of feelings too deep to be spoken of in other situations.

Then Phil slid over her, his body hard and soft and hot and made, it seemed, to fit hers, for he filled all the aching emptiness within her as they joined in the wild joy-ride of love.

Love-making, some remaining shred of common sense amended, but Maggie didn't care. This was Phil, taking her on a voyage of discovery of her own body and the sensual delights it could yield. And all the time he talked to her, sweet murmurs of allure, approval, passion and incitement, but never love, and although the final climax was momentous, leaving Maggie weak and trembling in his arms, that one small shred of common sense picked up that omission and clung to it, warning Maggie of just where she stood—or lay—in this relationship.

Phil was gone when Maggie woke on Monday morning. In her bed, not his. They'd shifted beds some time during the day, after foraging in the kitchen for food, and deciding Alex, as the landlord, had probably had the best bed in the house, and as it was now Maggie's bed, they were duty bound to try it.

Maggie felt a blush rising up from her toes as she thought of some of the other things they'd done, but it had all been fun, and the sex had been great, and they'd laughed in each other's arms and held onto each other as they'd slept.

'Like lovers!' Maggie whispered into the cold morning air. 'Which we are, of course,' she added, patting her stomach so the baby would know she was talking to it, and not think its mother was some nut who talked to herself.

And would continue to be, her head reminded her. After all, it would be stupid—not to mention hypocritical—to go on living in the same house and not continue to enjoy the physical delight they could offer each other. As Phil had pointed out some time yesterday, they'd already wasted two weeks.

She smiled at that and other memories, refused to think about the 'L' word that was absent from the equation and eased out of her nice warm bed. If she didn't get moving soon, she'd be late for work. Work! Had Phil been paged that he was already up?

She listened for noises in the house but heard none, and frowned, wondering why he hadn't woken her— let her know he was going.

No answer came to mind so she showered, blushing again at memories, dressed and went downstairs.

A note and a strange bouquet of leaves and berries from the garden were waiting for her on the kitchen table, the note explaining he had woken early and gone up to the hospital to get a start on the day, and apologising for the paucity of this floral offering, but it was all he'd been able to find so early in the morning.

Maggie smoothed the note with shaking fingers.

'Oh, Phil!' she whispered quietly. 'Don't be nice to me and make things harder than they already are.'

Then she wrapped her arms around her body and slumped down at the table.

He was so very much what she'd always wanted in a man, yet she was so wrong for him.

And because she loved him, she knew she couldn't marry him, condemning him to the loveless marriage his parents had endured.

Reminding herself there'd be no need to make any decisions if she lost this baby too, Maggie turned her thoughts to work. No paeds cardiac operations today, but she was scheduled to spend some time in another operating theatre, working in a supervisory capacity with some students doing their first paediatric anaesthetic.

She made toast and ate it with a glass of milk. She found milk nearly as revolting as tea, but she dutifully tried to drink some every day. Then she walked up the road to work, going straight to the paediatric ward where the children who would be her patients were waiting for her.

'We depend so much on patient weight in deciding the amount of drugs we give that if ever you have the slightest doubt about the weight of a child, weigh him or her again,' she told the three students. 'Ruby here is five and looks as if she might be light for her age, so the seventeen kilograms is probably right. Carry a weight-age chart so you can check if you need to, and when in doubt weigh.'

The students all nodded dutifully, then listened while Maggie explained to Ruby what she was going to do.

'I need to put a needle in the back of your hand so

the doctors can put medicine in there,' she told the little girl, already drowsy from the pre-med. 'Just a prick and we're done. You look at Mummy's face and see her scrunch it up when I put the needle in you. You watch and you'll think it's hurting her more than it's hurting you.'

While Ruby watched her mother who obligingly screwed up her face and said a loud 'Ouch!' Maggie sited a cannula in Ruby's hand and taped it into place.

'Ruby will be wheeled to Theatre by an orderly with a nurse accompanying her,' Maggie told the students. 'Because she's not on a ventilator, there's no need to bag her on the way, but with children who need oxygen, we bag them manually as they're moved. Although nurses usually do this, I like to go along with them.'

The orderly arrived to move the bed and Maggie, with the students trailing behind her, followed the little girl towards Theatre. Outside the door, Ruby's mother was asked to sign the consent form and agreed that, yes, it was her daughter going into Theatre and, yes, she was to have an appendicectomy.

Maggie was leading her crew into the changing rooms when a theatre sister who'd worked with the team a few times came out.

'Congratulations,' she said, beaming good-naturedly, then, as Maggie moved on, thinking the woman was talking to someone else, she thought she heard the sister add, 'He seems a great bloke, if something of a flirt.'

Puzzled, Maggie turned towards the two women students with her, but neither of them seemed to be responding to the conversation, and as the sister had, by now, disappeared from view, Maggie couldn't call her back to ask who she'd been talking to.

She found out later when, with Ruby and two other children safely out of the recovery room and back in their ward, she made her way to the rooms, hoping Annie might have been too tied up to eat lunch at the normal time and be willing to join her for a quick bite.

Annie wasn't in. In fact, apart from Becky, the rooms were empty. The secretary, who was usually full of good cheer, was obviously too busy for a chat, casting a glance towards Maggie then turning resolutely back towards the computer screen. So Maggie made her way down to the canteen alone.

'Oh, Maggie, I'm so glad for you.'

Annie was waiting for the lift on the ground floor and as Maggie stepped out, her colleague enveloped her in her arms and gave her a huge hug.

'It's so wonderful, being married, and I know you love Phil. I can't believe he's finally realised what a great woman you are. To think you've been there under his nose all this time while he played around with his blondes. Though I shouldn't be saying this, I know, but I really began to wonder about Phil—that he couldn't see just how good for him you'd be.'

Maggie, squashed in Annie's arms, took all this in, but her brain refused to process it.

Then the enormity of what Phil must have done struck her, and she was surprised she didn't self-combust so fiery was the anger that consumed her.

She broke away from Annie's embrace and opened her mouth to deny whatever lie Phil had spread, then saw the joy in her friend's face—joy that Maggie was sharing the happiness she and Alex had found—and knew she couldn't wipe that joy away.

Not now—not yet.

'Where is Phil?' she asked, hoping his name didn't come out as if she'd chewed broken glass before saying it.

'Just finishing lunch with Alex. He said you were busy today or we'd have waited.'

'I was busy,' Maggie said, stalled in the foyer outside the lift. She could hardly go into the canteen and rip Phil's head off—which was what she felt like doing—in front of Alex, and with this new news churning inside her, she doubted she could eat.

'And now I'm going home,' she said. 'Forgot to pick up the shopping list before I left this morning, and as I'm off this afternoon I may as well shop.'

Home indeed! she thought as she strode down the road. *It's a house, nothing more. The hide of the man, telling people we're engaged when I told him I wouldn't marry him.*

I did tell him, didn't I?

Yes, I'm sure I did.

Berating Phil, mentally at least, kept her moving quickly towards the house, but once there she had no idea why she'd come. She'd shopped on Saturday so certainly didn't need to shop again, but maybe she could pack her things and shift back to her sister's place.

But living there again, with her sister's four children, including two-year-old twins, might put her off children for life—right when she was hoping desperately to bring one into the world.

In thirty-something weeks...

Maybe...

Forget maybe, be positive!

'But with all that time ahead of us, why's Phil told people anything now?'

Even asked aloud, the question offered no answer, so Maggie went up to her bedroom, shut the door and collapsed onto the bed, staring at the ceiling and hoping some solution to her dilemma might just come to her.

Ripping off Phil's head still seemed the best solution, but some of her anger had dissipated by the time he came home later that afternoon, so all she did was yell.

'How dare you tell our colleagues we were engaged! I said no, Phil, remember, when you talked about marriage? No! No! No! Don't you understand the word?'

He looked dazed, as well he might, having breezed into the house with, this time, florist flowers in his hand, and an 'isn't life great' smile on his face, to be greeted by a small but furious woman.

'But I thought we'd established that yesterday,' Phil said lamely, offering the flowers then, realising they'd probably be flung at his head, dropping his hand back down so the bright blooms hung by his side.

'All we established yesterday,' an icy voice informed him, 'was that we were compatible in bed. Extremely compatible. Extraordinarily compatible if you like, but we probably suspected that from the first time. Marriage is more than compatibility in bed, Phil Park, and I would have thought even you were mature enough to have realised that!'

She wheeled away from him and stalked to the kitchen, her backside swaying so seductively it was all he could do not to scoop her up in his arms and take her back up to one or other of their bedrooms, where he could, he felt sure, sort the whole problem out in no time flat.

No, she thinks I should have some *maturity*, he reminded himself, but as no other solution offered itself, he followed her into the kitchen, allowing the fantasy to play in his mind.

'You'll have to tell everyone it's not true,' she told him as he entered, again proffering the flowers as if the second time around they might be more acceptable.

They weren't.

He set them down on the table and absorbed what she was saying.

'But why? Isn't marriage the best solution? Don't you think, as two mature adults, we can make a marriage between us work? Do you really want your baby to grow up with an absentee father?'

The last question snagged in his gut, and he had to protest it before she had time to answer.

'No, even if you do, that just wouldn't be acceptable to me, and as I'm half of the decision-makers here, I'm entitled to state that it won't happen. This baby will have two parents, both of whom live in the same house as he or she does, so there's absolutely no doubt in his or her mind who he or she belongs to.'

He got to the end of this appalling statement and realised why it had been so difficult, and why it probably didn't make sense.

'Should we give the baby a name now—some kind of unisex name like Mop or Gonk that we can refer to him or her by—so we don't have to keep saying he or she all the time?'

Maggie was staring at him as if he'd gone mad, but she didn't seem quite so angry. He considered trying the flowers again, then decided he was better off stopping while he was ahead so he crossed to the sink, searched under it until he found a jug, filled it with water and took it back to the table, where he picked up the flowers and stuck them into it.

'You should take them out of the paper, undo the string around them and cut off the bottom of the stems so they can take up fresh water,' the woman for whom they'd been intended said coolly, then she went to the fridge, took out the milk and some cheese, looked at both, put them back in, shut the door and sat down in a chair.

Suddenly.

So suddenly Phil looked more closely at her, and this time he didn't think of racing her off to bed.

'Have you eaten?' he demanded. 'Is that why you were at the fridge? Do you feel sick? If not, you have to eat. Even if you do feel sick, you have to eat. What? A cheese sandwich?'

He was so anxious and uncertain that Maggie had to laugh, and for a moment she thought how nice it would be to have Phil around all the time—bringing her flowers, fussing over her appetite...

Insidiously nice.

'I'll have a cheese sandwich. I'll get it in a minute. Just felt a bit woozy and thought it best to sit down.'

He fussed some more, insisting she stay sitting, scolding her for missing lunch, cutting the sandwich into little triangles and even finding a little bit of celery leaf to put on top so they looked appetising.

'And I'll make a pot of that decaff coffee,' he told her when he'd given her the sandwich. 'I know it's not like the real thing, but you probably need it, though you should drink it with milk to get some calcium.'

'Cheese has calcium,' she managed to say, although she had to swallow down a stupid lump of misery that had lodged in her throat—hormonal activity again, only this time it made her feel weepy for no other reason than that Phil was being nice to her.

But he was always nice to her, she reminded herself, chewing on the sandwich.

Not this kind of nice, herself said, although she knew this was a dangerous form of weakness, to be thinking of Phil's varying degrees of niceness and weeping over a cheese sandwich.

Especially when he didn't love her!

When it was all for the baby!

'None of this is making what you did right,' she told him when her body had been fortified and her will-power bolstered by the sandwich and a ghastly cup of milky coffee.

Phil was over at the sink, snipping the ends of the stems from the flowers. He turned his head towards her, his face serious—no twinkle in his eyes.

'No, if it's not what you want, then it isn't. I'm sorry.' He shrugged. 'I guess I can just tell Alex and Annie that we're not engaged—they'll spread the word.'

Maggie closed her eyes at the magnitude of *that* idea. Engaged one day, unengaged the next—the hospital gossips would have a ball and the grapevine would be buzzing with speculation.

She wasn't at all sure she could cope with the consequences. Not right now.

'Maybe not saying anything would be better. People might forget.'

'Of course,' Phil said politely, not meaning one word of it.

Neither did she, but a sudden wave of tiredness had swept over her and her brain had stopped working.

Maybe tomorrow she'd think of something...

CHAPTER NINE

BUT before tomorrow could come there was tonight.

Where would she be spending the night?

Where would Phil be?

She sighed, and he came and stood behind her and kneaded her shoulders, as she'd kneaded his about a hundred years ago.

'You should have something more substantial than a cheese sandwich for dinner,' he said, kneading in such a firm, unsexual way Maggie felt her whole body relaxing.

'I'm not hungry,' she said, and he didn't persist, shifting his attention to her neck, working magic on her knotted ligaments with his probing fingers.

'Then when I finish you should go to bed. Have a good night's sleep. Things always look better in the morning.'

'By morning the entire hospital will have heard we're engaged,' Maggie said bitterly. 'I can't see how that's going to make things look better.'

Phil kept kneading.

'Not necessarily. We're isolated from most of the hospital staff, being in the unit. And it's not as if, like Annie, you were on the staff at Jimmie's before the unit was set up. It's only our lot that have taken any notice of the news.'

Maggie had to agree, but she wasn't letting him off the hook that easily.

'And it's our lot that have to be told it isn't true. That it was a fabrication. We're not engaged, Phil.'

'But we *are* expecting a baby. And some time that's going to become obvious. What then? There's no way I'll have whispers about the little scrap's paternity. I'll make sure they know it's my baby you're expecting, Mags. And people will realise just how pig-headed you are at the same time.'

'Pig-headed?'

Maggie twisted away from his hands, and turned so she could glare up at him.

'You spread an untrue story through the hospital and *I'm* pig-headed because I want to tell the truth?'

He smiled, which was his first mistake.

The second was uttering the words that followed the smile.

'Too pig-headed to marry me. You know we'd be good together. Just because it wasn't your idea, you've got all uppity about it.'

Maggie stood up, still glaring at him, wishing she was a man so she could punch him and release just a little of the fury bubbling in her body.

'I wouldn't marry you if you were the last man on earth, Phil Park!' she yelled. Then she stormed out of the kitchen, across the living room, up the stairs and into her bedroom, where she flung herself on the bed and burst into tears.

Phil told himself he was having trouble getting through to Maggie because her hormones were out of kilter but, although he believed her hormones could well be causing havoc in her body, he couldn't help but feel there were other issues at stake here.

Things happening in Maggie's head that he had no inkling of.

He looked around the kitchen, wishing Minnie was there so he could talk things out with her, but she wasn't, so he checked the fridge instead, grabbed a light beer, then pulled out a piece of steak and the makings for a salad.

If they had a potato—and they had—he was set for dinner.

But grilling a steak, sticking a potato in the microwave and tossing salad ingredients with some oil and vinegar wasn't a difficult enough task to keep his mind from wandering. Salads were so healthy, but how did you get infants to eat lettuce? Or shouldn't you bother? Go with the tried and true mashed vegetables for a while, and introduce salad things when they could chew.

Obviously that would be best—you could hardly give a toothless baby a carrot stick.

So much to learn.

Was it too early to buy a baby book?

And what baby book to buy?

From what he'd seen in his sorties into book stores, bringing-up-baby books accounted for about half the store's turnover.

Maybe a quarter.

He couldn't ask his mother. He doubted she'd ever read one in her life, any more than his nanny had. Who did he know with offspring? Someone must know the best book to buy!

As he ate his meal his mind switched from the baby—plenty of time to find out about the best book— to the woman carrying it. Here he was eating the ultimate in healthy dinners and she'd gone to bed with only a cheese sandwich inside her. She'd wake up some time in the night absolutely starving.

Would she come downstairs if she was hungry, or should he leave a sandwich—there must be something other than cheese in the fridge—beside her bed?

Maggie was asleep when Phil crept in to her room, lying face down across the bed, still in her hospital clothes, the bedside lamp casting enough light for him to see the tear stains on her cheek.

His heart squeezed in his chest, but he ignored this physical manifestation of weakness. She was going through so much, he had to be the practical one.

He set the sandwich he'd made and covered with clingwrap on the table by the bed, but took the glass of milk back downstairs. He'd make her a hot chocolate, and bring it up, wake her and help her into her nightwear—professionally detached no matter if it killed him!—and encourage her to have the food and hot drink before she went back to sleep.

But by the time he returned, she'd gone, and he could hear the shower running in the bathroom. He left the drink beside the sandwich and departed. He'd made her cry once already this evening, he wasn't going to risk it again.

Maggie came out of the bathroom to find a cup of hot chocolate beside the sandwich, which had appeared while she'd been asleep.

She wasn't hungry and a skin was forming on the chocolate so that just looking at it made her feel ill, but he'd meant well.

He probably meant well about the baby, too, but there was no way she was going to mess up both their lives by marrying him.

She took the chocolate into the bathroom and tipped it down the sink, then eyed the sandwich. Maybe she should eat some of it. She mightn't want to marry him but there was no need to insult him further by not eating the food he'd so thoughtfully prepared. She forced it down, then slid into bed, turning her mind resolutely to work. What did they have on tomorrow? An ASD closure first up. Phil was doing it. The patient was a little girl who'd only recently been diagnosed, when she'd taken up horse-riding and had become so breathless after cantering gently around a paddock that the riding instructor had suggested her mother take her to a doctor.

Phil would go into the chest through a median incision—Scott would do that part—then Phil...

Always Phil, in her mind, in her dreams, in her heart...

The atmosphere in the theatre was relaxed and Maggie tried to work out why. Usually as the surgeons prepared a patient to go on bypass, the tension rose, not to an uncomfortable level but enough for everyone to feel it.

Was it because Rachel and Scott were teasing Phil about the end of his freedom? She opened her mouth to say that there was no end to his freedom, that they weren't engaged, then closed it again. This was not the time to be creating problems for Phil.

'Atrial septal defects—holes between the atria—aren't uncommon in congenital heart disease,' he was saying to the same students Maggie had instructed the previous day. 'The patient can be asymptomatic for years. Though blood is shunting from left to right across the atria, it isn't until they show signs of pulmonary obstruction, as little Gemma did, that the defect is discovered.'

'They'll close all by themselves quite often, won't they?' one of the students, a really beautiful young woman—blonde, of course—asked.

Maggie glared at her, but Phil didn't even turn in her direction, concentrating on attaching Gemma to the bypass machine and letting Scott answer for him.

'Yes, they do,' he said, then Kurt took over, explaining to the students how the bypass machine worked, acting as both heart and lungs for the patient while the operation was performed.

Maggie was listening to him and watching her monitors at the same time.

'She's fibrillating,' she said, knowing the panicky beat of the heart could lead to a heart attack if it wasn't stopped.

'The cannula's not seating properly, so she can't go on the pump yet,' Phil said, ordering the drugs Gemma needed to settle her heart back to an acceptable rhythm.

Maggie added them to the fluid flowing into the little girl, watching the monitor, not the child, willing the frantic beating of the heart to subside but not to stop.

'OK, go to pump, Kurt,' Phil said, and everyone breathed again.

'So much for a relaxed atmosphere in Theatre,' Maggie muttered, and Ned, the theatre sister who assisted in most of their operations, gave her a nudge with his elbow.

'You should know not to even think about such things in Theatre,' he said. 'It's tempting fate.'

Maggie wanted to agree with him but, though she nodded, her mind was back on the child. Had the problem been something she'd done? Had she added something to the cocktail of drugs immediately before the heart had gone haywire?

Later, when she read through the notes she made as she worked, she'd have to check if there was anything that could have triggered the reaction. She'd seen it happen before, but usually in very sick babies or neonates, not in otherwise healthy five-year-olds.

'That was unexpected,' Phil said, much later, when Gemma had been returned to the ward and they were gathered in the unit, discussing the operation.

'No change in your usual protocol?' Alex asked Maggie, who held up the notes she still had in her hand.

'Nothing!' she said. 'But it was scary and I'm wondering if there's something I don't know about in these cases where we're operating on an older and healthier child. I'll stay here tonight and trawl through whatever info I can find on the Web, and there's an anaesthetist over at Children's who's pretty savvy. He might have some ideas.'

She noticed Phil's scowl but thought nothing of it until he announced, late that afternoon when she settled in front of the computer, that he, too, would stay back and do some Web surfing.

'But your work was textbook,' Maggie reminded him. 'I've seen Alex do ASDs and he couldn't have done it better. And the fibrillation was so early in the procedure, I don't see how it could have been caused by anything you did.'

'I'd still like to know if there's any paper or report of something similar happening,' he said, sounding so grouchy she decided to leave him alone.

Maggie was reading through an article on possible reactions between some pre-medications and the use of pain relief during surgery when a cheery voice interrupted her concentration.

'Two of you hard at work,' Evan Knowles said.

'And I bet you haven't eaten, Maggie. I missed lunch and I'm starving, so how about you guide me to this canteen of yours and we'll eat and talk? Phil can mind the computers.'

'Phil hasn't eaten either,' Maggie said, darting a quick glance in Phil's direction and catching a scowl as a reward.

She ignored it and continued, 'Come on, Phil, we'll all go and eat. We can talk to Evan over dinner—he might have some experience of what happened.'

Evan looked put out, Phil looked thunderous, and Maggie wondered why women ever put up with men! But eventually he stood up and, still glowering, took Maggie's arm and all but frogmarched her out of the room.

Evan walked on her other side, chatting on, either unaware of the vibes around him or choosing speech as a way of ignoring them.

'Oh, Maggie, I was hoping to see you.'

One of the nurses who cared for their patients on the open ward was waiting by the lift. 'I saw Phil yesterday and congratulated him, but I didn't see you. All the best on your engagement.'

'We're not engaged.'

The words came out before Maggie had time to consider the company—or the impact they would have on the two men standing next to her.

'You're engaged?'

That from Evan, who'd spoken too early to hear her denial.

'What happened to not saying anything?'

This from Phil, frowning down at her from what suddenly seemed like a great height.

The nurse looked embarrassed, muttered something about forgetting to check a list and hurried off.

'It was a misunderstanding,' Maggie said, mainly to Evan although the answer could equally apply to Phil's protest.

'Oh, yes,' Evan said, looking from one to the other. 'Happens all the time, I imagine, one half of a couple thinking they're engaged while the other half thinks they're not. Ordinary kind of misunderstanding!'

Maggie laughed.

'It's complicated,' she said, and Evan sighed.

'More so than you realise,' he said quietly. 'Anyway, I wanted to see young Pete while I was here, so how about you two eat on your own? Maggie, I'll check out some likely sites for anything about your problem and email you.'

He walked off before Maggie had a chance to stop him.

'Now see what you've done,' she said to Phil.

'I've done?' he echoed with totally false astonishment. 'I had nothing to do with it—it was the nurse who mentioned engagements.'

'And she'd have known if you hadn't told the world?' Maggie stormed at him, wanting to yell but knowing this wasn't the place for a really good argument.

Then Phil smiled at her, and all her anger melted.

'I know it's a terrible cliché, but you look beautiful when you're angry. Your cheeks go pink and your eyes spark fire, and all I want to do is kiss you.'

He spoke quietly, although they were now alone, the other people waiting with them having taken the lift.

'Phil, this is all wrong,' Maggie said. 'There's so much more to it—things I haven't told you.' Her stom-

ach scrunched but she forced herself to add, 'Things
that will probably make the engagement unnecessary.'

She knew it wasn't the ideal place to tell Phil about
her previous marriage and two miscarriages, but it was
time things were said, and she was ready to say them,
so—

'Phil, Maggie, I think you should see Pete.'

Evan's voice betrayed his urgency and Phil and
Maggie responded immediately, turning and striding
towards the unit's PICU.

'He was fine, breathing well on his own with the
machine assisting him, but he wasn't reliant on it, so
we decided to try him off it,' the intensivist on duty
explained. 'We intended keeping him on ventilatory
assistance but getting him off the mechanical ventilator, so he's been fasting today in preparation for it and
we cut his fluids right back, but there's obviously fluid
collecting in his abdomen.'

The little boy, though awake, was far from alert,
lying limply on the bed, his usual cheery smile no-
where to be seen.

'So, not feeling too good, soldier?' Phil said, while
Maggie nodded to Mr Barron, on duty by his son's
bedside today. Mr Barron called his youngster 'soldier'
and most of the staff had adopted it, pleasing Pete enor-
mously.

But today he didn't respond at all, just lying there
while Phil poked and prodded at his body.

Let it not be kidney failure, Maggie prayed, then she
reminded herself that Pete's kidneys weren't being
overworked as he still had a drain in his abdomen and
he was undergoing peritoneal dialysis.

Peritoneal dialysis! Her mind raced through what she
knew of it. Usually done during the night while the

patient slept, it was a way of cleansing the impurities from the blood and adding needed electrolytes, performing the tasks of the kidneys when they were too weak to function properly.

But one of the dangers of it was peritonitis, an infection getting into the abdomen through the catheters designed to keep the body healthy.

Phil was explaining some of this to Mr Barron, whose complexion had gone from a healthy, if somewhat ruddy olive to a dull, tired grey—a skin colour seen quite often in the exhausted family members of PICU patients.

Only, as well as grey skin, there was a blue tinge to Mr Barron's lips.

'Phil,' Maggie said, intending to nod towards the man in case Phil hadn't noticed, but it was too late. Mr Barron pitched forward off his chair, and little Pete's weak but frantic cry of 'Dad!' was one of the saddest things Maggie had ever heard.

She didn't hesitate, hitting the crash button in the room. Although the closest crash cart would be geared towards paediatric resuscitations, it would be better than nothing for Mr Barron.

Maggie moved around the bed, stepping over Phil who, with Evan, was giving CPR to the prone man, and stood so Pete could no longer see what was going on.

'Daddy's just fainted,' she lied to the sick little boy. 'Probably because Dr Phil was talking about such yucky things.'

But the monitors showed Pete's agitation and Maggie sent a nurse for a mild sedative. Just a little of the drug, added to what he was already on, would make him sleepy and unaware of what was happening, at least until they could move his father out of the room.

Better that way than having the already ill little boy deal with the chemicals his body would produce through anxiety.

He slipped peacefully into sleep, but Maggie stayed by his side. Someone else would contact Mrs Barron, who would then have to make arrangements for a friend or relative to mind the other children before she could get up to the hospital.

Mr Barron was defibrillated where he lay on the floor, and the collective sigh of relief told Maggie he'd responded. Within minutes of his collapse he was lifted onto a stretcher and wheeled out of the room, Phil and Evan following, the intensivist obviously wanting to go too, though he did turn back towards Maggie to check that Pete was OK.

'I knocked him out,' she explained. 'I'll stay with him because when he comes to again he'll want to know his dad's all right, and we still have to sort out his problem.'

She sat down and reached for Pete's hand, stroking it and talking to him as she waited for him to wake. No one really knew how much an anaesthetised person could take in, but Maggie believed some words filtered into the other world the patient temporarily inhabited, so she always talked to them as they came out of anaesthetic.

She told Pete he was going to get better, that they'd fight the infection, and before long he'd be going home to play with his sisters and brothers. She crossed her fingers again as she added, 'And your mother and father, too, of course.'

Phil walked back into the PICU and hesitated outside

Pete's room, looking through the glass at the woman who sat beside the child's bed, holding his hand and talking away, although Pete appeared to be comatose.

'You could have gone and had your dinner,' he told her, coming into the room and nodding towards the sleeping child.

'And leave him on his own—when his parents have been knocking themselves out to make sure someone's with him all the time?'

She smiled at Phil.

'And why did you come back? To sit with him, I bet!'

'To check on him, that's all. Though I might have known you'd be here—persistence personified, that's you.'

He knew she was still annoyed with him, but reached out to ruffle her hair anyway.

'It might be an irritating trait to your friends and family, but it pays off in your work, Mags. You worry away at things until you find not only a right solution but a perfect solution.'

As she hadn't objected to his touch, he dropped his hand onto her shoulder.

She didn't bite it off, which cheered him immensely, not because it was his operating hand but because she must be over the argument and they could be friends again.

Friends! More and more he was realising the importance of this friendship between them—valuing it, treasuring it...

Wanting it to continue.

He reined in his wandering thoughts, returning to the problem at hand.

'Though I doubt even you can find a perfect solution

to the Barron family's dilemma. Five children, one still desperately ill after major surgery, and the prospect of more surgery to come, and now the father in the coronary care unit.'

Maggie looked up at him and smiled.

'Have faith,' she said, 'but speaking of the Barrons' problems, how is Mr B.?'

'He should pull through. He's a bit overweight, but he's relatively young. The worry isn't the first heart attack, but the likelihood of a second.'

'And then a probably fatal third!' Maggie finished for him. 'Though surely, with drugs, and possibly a lifestyle change, the second and third can be averted.'

Phil nodded, his eyes now on Pete's monitors, which were showing a drop in the oxygen saturation in his blood. He touched the computer, then brought up the drug schedule. The intensivist had already given antibiotics for the peritonitis, but they'd take time to work.

'The fluid in his abdomen must be pressing his diaphragm upwards and compromising his lungs. I'm going to have to draw off some of the fluid. I'll need some for testing anyway,' he said. 'It might be easier on him to do it while he's still sleeping. How long have I got?'

Maggie looked at her watch, calculated the amount of drug she'd given Pete, his weight, other medications he was on and gave an estimate of fifteen minutes.

Phil asked the nurse who'd followed him into the room for the equipment he'd need, then with Maggie still holding Pete's hand and talking to him, and with the nurse assisting, he drew off two large syringes of fluid, putting some into smaller vials and sending them off to the pathology lab.

'Do you know if they have Dial an Angel or a similar organisation here in Sydney?' Maggie asked, but before he'd even made sense of the question, she answered it herself.

'No, of course you wouldn't. Probably don't even know what Dial an Angel is.'

'I do, so. It's an organisation that provides help for people who need it, mainly in the house, help with kids and housework and suchlike. But if you're thinking of it for the Barrons, and your organisation is like ours, it's probably not affordable for them.'

'No, but there are ways and means,' Maggie said, smoothing her hand up and down Pete's thin arm.

She looked up at Phil.

'If you're finished here, could you send Annie in— if she's still in the rooms, that is? She'll know how to go about things.'

Phil hadn't a clue what she was up to but he had finished, and as Maggie seemed to have no intention of leaving to have dinner with him, or for any other reason, he may as well go and talk to Annie.

He was at the door before she asked the question he'd expected earlier.

'Where's Evan?'

'He had to go,' Phil said, and hoped Maggie wouldn't pursue it. Hoped so much he nearly crossed his fingers as he had done when wishing for something as a child.

Not pursue it! This was Maggie!

'Go where? And why?'

'Back to the Children's, I guess, and why, because he's a worker like the rest of us. He probably had a child waiting to go under even while he was over here dallying with you.'

'It's eight o'clock at night, so an op's unlikely, and

he came so we could talk about the anaesthetic,'
Maggie reminded him. 'Though when I phoned, he said
he was coming anyway, wanting to see Pete and talk
to him about pain.'

'Well, there you are,' Phil said, delighted Maggie
had handed him an excuse. 'With Pete so ill, then his
father collapsing, Evan probably felt he was in the way
here at Jimmie's.'

Maggie nodded, and though it didn't seem to be a
nod of total acceptance Phil took it as such and slipped
away.

It wasn't as if he'd thumped the man, he comforted
himself as he walked through to their rooms. All he'd
done had been to let slip the information that he and
Maggie *were* engaged, though he was in trouble for
telling people before her family had thrown them a
party and made an official announcement.

He'd felt slightly guilty, feeding Knowles this lie,
though not about the lie, more about the fact he knew
absolutely nothing about Maggie's family, and didn't
even know if they'd want to give a party or make official announcements.

He had a feeling such arrangements, like the man
asking the woman's father for her hand in marriage,
were things of the past.

Annie had already heard the news of Mr Barron's
collapse, and agreed that something needed to be done
to help the family.

'I don't see what you can do,' Phil told her, but she
bustled off to see Maggie anyway.

Maggie was excited. Annie knew just the right organisation to contact to arrange help for the Barrons, and
though they'd agreed to wait until one of them had

talked to Mrs Barron before making final arrangements Annie had gone off to find out exactly what was available.

'But you're his anaesthetist, you shouldn't have had to sit with him,' Mrs Barron said to her as she came anxiously into Pete's room.

'I wanted to,' Maggie told her, 'and I wanted to talk to you as well.'

She indicated the little boy, now sleeping naturally and less flushed as well, a sure sign the antibiotics were clearing the infection.

'I knew you'd come to see Pete once you were satisfied Mr Barron was in good hands, so I stayed on.'

She pulled the second chair close to the one she was using, then swapped places so Mrs Barron could hold her son's hand.

'We all know the trouble you've had juggling your family at home with the hospital visits and Mr Barron's work, and with this, you must be nearly frantic.'

Mrs Barron smiled at her.

'I don't think frantic comes anywhere close,' she said, blinking away a tear. 'I know I have to be strong because so many people are depending on me, but I've always depended on Joe. He's been my rock. I'd never have got through all the problems little Pete's had without Joe being there, telling me all the time we've got to see it through.'

Maggie put her arms around the other woman and let her cry for a while, then, as Mrs Barron straightened, Maggie told her about the charitable organisation that could arrange support for her.

'It has to be what *you* want,' she said. 'Help that will make things easy for *you*. It could be a live-in person to take care of the kids or someone to come in to clean and cook. Someone to drive you to and from the hospital, or money for taxis, someone to drive the kids to school if you like. Whatever you need, these people will give it to you until you've got Joe back home again. After that, too, if you need support for a little while.'

Mrs Barron looked at Maggie as if she'd gone mad.

'But there are loads of people in the world far, far worse off than us. I've got Mum, who will come and stay, and while I know doing everything will be too much for her, it gives me peace of mind to know she's there. Joe, too—he wouldn't like to think a stranger was with the kids.'

'Then maybe someone to clean and cook, do the washing and ironing and leave your mother free to see to the children. Would you accept that?'

Mrs Barron nodded, but she was frowning mightily.

'Why us?' she asked, and Maggie smiled at her.

'Because you need help and you need it now. Think about it, about what would help.'

Maggie watched her face and knew she was weakening.

'If someone could come in the morning at eight and take the kids to school, then give Mum a hand around the house, I could spend the nights at the hospital and stay with Joe and Pete in the mornings, then go home in time to collect the kids. That way I can give them time in the afternoons and see to their homework, and fix their lunches for the next day.'

She looked at Maggie.

'Are you sure these people exist? And they're free?'

'They exist, and while they charge for their services, the organisation will pay, not you. We'll make sure we get someone with a car big enough for all the children and your mother, because you'll both feel better if she goes in the car to the school the first week or so.'

'Week or so? They might come for more than a week?'

Mrs Barron began to cry again, and as Maggie comforted her, holding the weeping woman and patting her on the back, she raised her eyes to the ceiling beyond which she still believed heaven existed, and said a quiet thank you.

Big miracles, like getting Pete and Mr Barron better immediately, were beyond her but, thanks to what had been a tragic loss ten years ago, small miracles were within reach.

CHAPTER TEN

'COME on, I'm taking you home.'

Maggie looked up from the computer and pushed her fingers through her hair. Her earlier high, when she and Annie had arranged for an 'angel' to help out at the Barrons', had disappeared, mainly because her search for something similar to what had happened today had proved fruitless. All she'd found out was that peering at the screen for an hour gave her a pain in the neck.

'I don't know!' she complained to Phil. 'Computers are good, but they can also lead you on endless wild-goose chases. I'd pick up something in search results that sounded similar and follow it through, only to find it was a different matter entirely—fibrillation in octogenarian patients or fibrillation as a result of metabolic disturbance.'

He'd come closer and rested his hand on her shoulder as he, too, peered at the screen. Any of their colleagues would have done the same thing, but only Phil's touch warmed her skin and eased the stiffness in her neck.

Until she realised why he was so interested in the information on the computer—not fibrillation at all. Frustrated at not finding anything similar to what had happened with Gemma, Maggie had run a quick search on personal medical matters, and although the search engine hadn't delivered any results when Phil had first walked in, they were all up on the screen now—page one of one hundred and eighty-four—all concerning spontaneous abortion in the first trimester of a pregnancy.

Phil's grip tightened on her shoulder and he crouched beside her.

'You haven't lost the baby, have you? Today? You shouldn't be here. Why didn't you say something?'

He was so pale and seemed so upset Maggie stopped any further speculation by putting her hand across his mouth.

'I haven't lost the baby,' she told him, then hesitated, took a deep breath and added, 'but I might. That's why I really didn't want to say anything, Phil. To you or to anyone else. Back when I was still a student, I was married. Jack was my first boyfriend—we'd been together at school, then at uni, we got married, I got pregnant...'

'You lost the baby?' Phil guessed, hoping he sounded OK when in reality his mind and body were coping with some strange reactions to the news Maggie had once been married.

Surely that hot, tight sensation in his gut couldn't be jealousy!

And coming on top of the shock discovery—however wrong—that she'd lost the baby, it was almost too much to cope with right now!

He decided to ignore all the internal commotion going on and concentrate on what she was telling him.

'That one and the next. But by the time I lost the second one I wasn't married any more, and I was also determined to get back on track with my career, so I didn't do anything about investigating why it had happened.'

She hesitated and Phil could read the fear lurking in her dark eyes, and again experienced a physical tightening of his gut—though this time for Maggie, for how she must be feeling.

'Now I wish I had,' she whispered. 'Wish I'd found out if there was some reason why I miscarried twice. Wish I knew if it was likely to happen again...'

Phil eased up from his crouched position and put his arms around her, drawing her to her feet so he could hold her properly and offering her the warmth and comfort of his body.

But while physically he was offering comfort, mentally he was nearly as upset as she was. They might lose this baby? That would be bad enough, but with no baby there'd be no reason for Maggie to marry him, and that thought bothered him more than the losing-the-baby possibility.

So, they'd better not lose the baby.

'Did you find anything? On the computer?'

Maggie obviously understood what he meant, for she pushed away from him.

'You saw the screen—the results have just come up. I hadn't looked at anything, let alone found anything.'

Phil heard the strain in her voice and pulled her close again, thinking now of practical matters.

'About a million hours ago, we were on our way to the canteen for dinner. Did you ever eat?'

She shook her head against his chest.

'I got over being hungry.'

'Me, too, but that's not good for either of us. Let's close this computer down, order something nutritious and delicious to be delivered, and go home. By the time we get there, the food will be on its way. We'll eat then go to bed. We can do a search tomorrow.'

He tilted her chin so he could look into her eyes.

'We could even consult an obstetrician—there's sure

to be a couple somewhere around the hospital. But for now let's go home.'

'Now *you're* saying the word,' she said, to hide the melting sensation in her bones his 'let's go home' had caused.

He smiled.

'Home? I guess I am—and do you know what, Mags? It feels like home. Or it does when we're not at odds with each other.'

He brushed his lips against her forehead and crossed to Annie's desk, where a list of all the local restaurants that delivered food was taped on the outside of the hospital phone directory.

'Italian?'

Maggie nodded. She was still absorbing what he'd said about their house feeling like a home and telling herself not to get too excited about it. He'd already told her he could feel 'at home' wherever he was working.

'Delivery in three-quarters of an hour. That will give us time to pop in on Pete before we leave—if you don't mind.'

They walked briskly through to the PICU, and Phil, rather than disturb the sleeping boy, or his mother who was dozing in the big chair by the bed, stopped at the desk and checked the monitor to see how his charge was doing.

'Temp's down, oxygen sats up, more fluid building in his abdomen, but we'll drain some more off during the night if it affects either his heart or his lungs,' the intensivist who'd joined Phil at the desk said.

They were turning away when Mrs Barron came out.

'Oh, Dr Walsh, I wanted to thank you again for the angel. I visited Joe and he was conscious but worrying, and as soon as I told him about the angel, the nurse said all his readings got better.'

She gave Maggie a hug, sniffed back a tear and beamed at Phil.

'This is some woman you've got yourself,' she said, then she returned to continue her vigil by her son's bed.

'Angel?' Phil queried as they went down in the lift.

'Annie and I arranged some home help for Mrs Barron, so she's not worrying herself to death about the family at home while she's visiting the hospital.'

'Most places I've worked, it could take weeks to organise home help. Unless, of course, you've got the wherewithal to pay for it, which I doubt is the case for the Barrons.'

'There are ways and means,' Maggie told him, not wanting to get into those particular ways and means.

'What ways and means?'

So much for not wanting to get into it.

'Annie and I are ''locals''—well, she's a local and I'm from Melbourne, but it's the same country and a number of the same organisations exist in all the states.'

'You're waffling!'

They'd reached the hospital exit and Maggie stopped to pull on a jacket, Phil once again taking it from her hands and holding it for her to put on.

He couldn't resist the urge to hug her, once again wrapping his arms around her bulky, jacketed figure and drawing her close to his body. Then he freed her and in case she thought he'd lost the track of the conversation, he gave it a nudge.

'Ways and means?'

'I know this charitable trust that does small things like pay for home help in emergency situations. Annie found the helper and I'm arranging the finance for it. That's all.'

He was sure it wasn't all, but she wouldn't tell him more—not until she was ready. She was as stubborn as she was persistent, his Mags.

His Mags? Now, where had that come from?

The food arrived soon after they got home, and they sat together in the kitchen, eating what was now a very late dinner.

'I was hungrier than I realised,' Maggie said, tucking into a bowl of pasta with a chicken and pesto sauce, taking a break occasionally to help herself to some salad as well.

'Eating for two,' Phil teased, then regretted it when he saw the fear in her eyes. Fear for this baby, or remembered fear?

A different fear clutched at Phil's heart. Annie, they now knew, had lived in fear of an abusive husband, and with reason as the man had found and shot her, luckily only wounding her. Was this Maggie's fear as well?

'What happened, Maggie, that you weren't married any more when you had the second miscarriage?'

She looked surprised, then frowned and toyed with her fork, twirling it in the bowl.

'We'd known each other for ever, it seemed,' she said quietly. 'At school and then at uni—Jack doing engineering, me medicine. He wasn't well and we put it down to exhaustion. He was working part time as well—we both were—so he didn't see a doctor soon enough. He had leukaemia, acute, the prognosis terrible because it had been discovered too late. What he wanted most was to leave something behind. Something of himself—a child to go on living for him. We got married and I fell pregnant before he began radiation treatment, and just to be safe we also had some sperm frozen so if anything happened with the first pregnancy I could have another go.'

'And you miscarried twice!'

Phil took her hand and held it, his heart aching with pity for the young student she had been.

'He died?'

Maggie nodded.

'He died before he knew I'd lost the second baby. That was the only good thing—the timing of the loss. He died thinking the baby was OK and he'd live on in his son.'

She raised her head and offered a watery smile to Phil.

'Silly man—he was so sure it would be a son!'

'And you didn't try again. Didn't want to, later on?'

Maggie shook her head.

'I can't make myself believe that dead people know what's happening back on earth. I like the idea of a heaven, but I'm a doctor. I believe people live on in the memories of those who loved them, and in the people whose lives were touched by them, or are still touched in some way. Jack lives on that way.'

'Jack still touches people's lives?'

Maggie's face cleared of the grief he'd seen wash across it.

'He does,' she said simply, then she smiled at Phil. 'He's the charitable institution I talked about earlier. The one that will pay for the Barrons' angel. Jack's Way, it's called, because he always believed you should show people how you feel about them in a practical way.'

She hesitated but Phil wanted—needed?—to know more.

'Go on,' he encouraged, and won another smile, this one slightly embarrassed.

'It's funny to think how young we were!' Maggie said softly, still smiling.

Then she looked into Phil's eyes.

'When we were students, first and second year, we spent so much time sitting around talking, nearly always putting the world to rights. Were you the same? I imagine most young people are. Anyway, Jack maintained you should do what you can to help others who were trying to help themselves. Helping themselves was the important part. People who didn't try—who just took whatever they could get from government agencies or charities—infuriated Jack, but real battlers, well, he always had time for them.'

'So Jack's Way helps out battlers?' Phil prompted. He wasn't sure he wanted to know any more about this obviously saintly husband, but at the same time he was learning more about Maggie than he ever had before. 'Do you fundraise? How did you set it up?'

Maggie ate another piece of chicken then pushed her bowl away.

'He had a huge life insurance policy. Neither of us knew that, but his father had taken it out when Jack was young, thinking he could eventually cash it in when he wanted to buy a house. The last thing anyone expected was that a young healthy man would die.'

She paused and Phil waited.

'I didn't want the money,' she added in a small voice, 'so, with some friends, we founded Jack's Way and now every year the university students' union puts money into it as well, so we don't ever have to touch the principal but can use interest and donations to fund things like some help for the Barrons. We tend to do the small stuff that big agencies don't handle—things that don't cost much but, because we can put help in place immediately, can make a tremendous difference for families in times of crisis.'

Phil shook his head.

'What else have you done?'

Radiance shone through her smile this time.

'We've done the most amazing things, but they're simple things really. Flying a woman to South America after her daughter was injured in a car accident, bringing a grandmother out from England to take care of a suddenly orphaned family, paying for a young boy who'd lost his legs to go to the US for special prosthetics. We don't publicise the donations or help we give, but the larger agencies know about us, and hospitals in Melbourne are aware we exist, so somehow people in need seem to find us. It's confidential, the help we give—no, anonymous is probably a better word. I've only talked to you about it because of the Barrons.'

'And because you wanted to think about something other than miscarriages?' Phil said, reaching out to take her hand. 'Come on, it's very late. Let's go to bed. My bed, so I can hold and comfort you. It's way too late for anything but sleep. OK?'

Maggie looked at him, aware that the relationship between them had shifted into a different dimension.

Whether for better or worse, she wasn't sure, but she knew with the ghosts she'd raised this evening still floating around her head, her own bed would have been a very sad and lonely place.

But...

'Phil, I don't think that's a good idea. Going to bed with you—continuing a physical relationship...' She paused and even managed a smile. 'And don't tell me we wouldn't get physical no matter how late it is. It's just going to make things harder in the end.'

'In what end?' he asked, looking genuinely puzzled.

'In the end when we say that it's over.'

'But why need it be over? Why will this end come? We're good together, Mags, and be positive—we'll have the baby. And more babies to keep the little scrap company—that's if you want more babies—'

Maggie held up her hand to stop him talking before he dug himself into more trouble. She knew she'd reached the stage where only the truth would do, but she was so used to keeping all her feelings bottled up inside her she found it hard to put them into words.

'Being good together isn't enough for me, Phil. I married once for convenience. Oh, I loved Jack dearly and would have done anything for him—marrying him was no sacrifice. But if I marry again, it has to be for love. Not because I'm pregnant.'

She looked into the blue eyes of the man who'd sneaked in under her guard and stolen her heart, and saw confusion and more than a little pain. Standing up, she moved around the table and bent to kiss him on the cheek.

'I love you, Phil, but one-sided love's a desperate, lonely place to be. Let's wait and see about the baby, then make arrangements when and if we need to.'

It was as good an exit line as any, she thought as she walked out of the kitchen, her unfinished meal still on the table.

It was Phil's job to clear away and stack the dishwasher anyway, she told herself, as she dragged her weary body up the bed.

And you will not cry, she added silently. Not tonight and not any night. Your hormones aren't in that much of a mess.

But waking in the morning, she found her pillow strangely damp and realised her willpower hadn't worked while she'd slept.

The house was empty, a note from Phil saying he'd gone to work early tucked under the vase of flowers she'd never thanked him for.

Phil found her in the small lounge off the theatre, writing up notes on the operation they'd completed earlier. She hadn't heard him come in, and he watched her for a few seconds, the words she'd said last night echoing in his head.

He'd thought of Maggie as self-contained—right from when he'd first met her—but was that self-containment a cover for the lonely place she spoke of? Had she loved someone else who hadn't loved her? Someone after Jack?

Or was he, Phil, the one who'd sent her into exile there?

She'd said she loved him but there'd been despair in her words, and it had been that despair that had haunted him throughout the night.

Oh, she'd mentioned love earlier—even, if he remembered rightly, asked if he could offer it to her. But he'd brushed it aside, thinking love was connected with his dream—thinking about his version of what love might be, not what he might gain from giving it.

But if he said that now, told her he loved her as

Maggie and she was more important to him than any childhood dream, would she believe it?

Probably not! He was finding it hard to believe himself—this tumultuous shift in his emotions.

So rather than rush into action as he had already—engagement announcements and flowers, to name but two incidents—he had better make sure he explained what he was feeling in a very convincing manner.

And at an appropriate time…

Which wasn't right now.

He moved towards her, speaking quietly.

'I've made an appointment for us to see the obstetrician at four. He has rooms on the sixth floor—six-four-seven.'

She looked up and frowned, as if trying to place him, then she shook her head.

'You know once a woman's pregnant it's too late to do any tests to find out why she might have miscarried previously? All an obstetrician will say is wait and see.'

'But between eight and twelve weeks you can have a scan to date the baby's birth—I was reading up on it last night. They do a measurement called CRL—crown-rump length—and from a scale can tell exactly when it's due. Great, isn't it?'

He'd been fascinated by the things he'd learnt but Maggie didn't seem to be sharing his fascination. In fact, her frown seemed to have grown deeper.

'I'm not having a scan,' she said firmly.

'But—'

'No, Phil, I'm not! Neither am I seeing an obstetrician—not yet.'

She sighed, then closed the book she had beside the file on the coffee-table.

'Look, I may not have sought medical advice about

why I'd miscarried twice or had tests done, but I was a med student, for heaven's sake. I *did* look into it. If you want facts and figures, twenty per cent of pregnant women miscarry—that's one in five—most too early to recognise it as a miscarriage. Usually it's because of a foetal abnormality but occasionally it's a physical problem. The woman has an infection, there are environmental factors like smoking and drinking or even stress, which I was certainly suffering at the time. Then there are endocrine disorders.'

She sighed.

'The list goes on, Phil, but without knowing the exact cause, the best obstetrician in the world wouldn't be able to do anything right now.'

Maggie watched him, hoping this was sinking in—hoping mostly that he'd just walk away.

But hope didn't seem to be on her side right now. He came closer to sit on the couch beside her.

'I understand all of that, but why no obstetrician appointment? Why no scan?'

She turned to face him, then turned away again, her hand moving to protect her stomach. Then dipped her head so he wouldn't read the pain she felt in her face.

'Because having it confirmed—worse, seeing it on a scan—would make the baby so much more real. I'm sorry, but, knowing I might lose it, I can handle things—just—the way they are. But if I see its shape—at eight weeks it's got a face, Phil, the beginning of features, even a chin—no, I don't want to know this baby that intimately, thank you.'

The final words croaked out past all the emotional turmoil in her chest, but she got them said. Whether Phil understood or not, she didn't know and tried not to care.

But she did care, wanting his understanding nearly as much as she longed for his love.

Surely understanding wasn't too much to ask for...

'Ah, glad to find the two of you together. We're in strife—we as in the unit—and Alex wants to talk to the whole team in the rooms a.s.a.p.'

Had Annie, standing in the doorway, heard their conversation? She looked concerned but she would be, if the continuation of the unit was at risk.

'We'll be right with you.'

Phil answered for both of them, but though Maggie rose immediately to her feet he was slower, taking his time, waiting until Annie had departed then pulling Maggie into his arms and holding her close.

'It's your call, Mags,' he said softly. 'Whatever you want. Whatever it's in my power to give you. I mean that.'

She held him close for a moment, then pushed away, looking up into his face.

'Except love,' she reminded him.

And it was too late for him to tell her.

Love was forgotten as they joined the team, propped against desks in the suite of rooms, no one sitting down, which seemed strange. Until they learned of a medical negligence case being brought against the hospital following the death of Dr Ellis's patient.

Bad news apparently required you to be upright when you heard it!

'Are we mentioned specifically in the charge? Me? The unit?' Phil asked.

Alex shook his head.

'The charge is against the hospital but although it could take years to get to court, the hospital is taking it seriously and moving towards palliative—if that's the word in law as well as medicine—measures now.'

'Like blaming us and closing the unit?'

Rachel asked the question in all their minds.

'Something like that,' Annie explained. 'That way, when the case comes to court, or if they decide to go to mediation, the hospital can say, well, the problem was within this trial unit we'd set up, and we've now disbanded it so it won't happen again. A copout.'

'But the hospital would still have to pay if negligence is proved,' Maggie put in.

'The hospital has insurance, we all have insurance, it's only the insurance companies who pay,' Rachel said.

'Yes, they'll make the actual pay-out—part with the money—but they're also the ones who'll look for someone else to blame,' Kurt told her. 'The hospital's insurance company will come gunning for the unit, or for the insurance company that provides cover for the unit members.'

'But they have to prove negligence,' Annie said. 'Maybe we're getting all worked up over nothing.'

'They can't and won't prove negligence against us,' Alex said grimly. 'Phil made the absolutely correct decision, but don't tell me the administrators wouldn't prefer us as the scapegoat rather than Dr Ellis. After all, they'll figure most of the current unit staff will be gone before the case comes to court. Other hospital interests have already been clamouring to have both our funding and our theatre. They can offer a sop to the complainant's solicitors and placate their own departments all at once.'

'But if they use us as a scapegoat it will tarnish your and Phil's reputations. Phil's specifically,' Kurt pointed out. 'There's no way we can accept some kind of compromise or be shuffled quietly off into the sunset to give them something to offer to the other side's solicitors.'

'I could leave.'

Maggie knew she wasn't the only one who'd been struck dumb by Phil's pronouncement, but she was probably the only one whose heart stopped beating.

'Nonsense!'

Annie put everyone's feelings into one succinct word, but Phil held up his hand before anyone else could object.

'No, listen to me. It's the only sensible solution. If I get out, the team's reputation remains untarnished.'

'But yours…'

Rachel moved to stand beside him, unable to put her argument into words but wanting to show support.

'There's no way I'd allow that,' Alex said, also moving a little closer to his friend and colleague.

Maggie watched and wondered if any of them had noticed their physical reactions—if they were aware of moving closer to Phil.

She was by his side anyway, but had never felt further away. She had no idea what to say or do, but her heart, which had resumed beating, now ached with a weary kind of confusion. Was it because she was standing next to Phil that she sensed the pain his words had caused him? Or was it because she loved him and love had unconsciously discovered all the little nuances in his voice, and speech, and movements?

'You wouldn't have to allow it, Alex,' Phil said quietly. 'I'd resign.'

'You're not through your fellowship,' Alex said, angry now. 'And you'd be letting me down—and the whole team. We *are* a team, remember, and we stick together.'

'Scott can take my place. He's not had the experience, but he's going to be very good. Possibly better than me. For difficult cases, you can always get someone over from Children's. It's the way things were done here before—a paeds cardiac surgeon from over there, helping one of the adult surgeons from here.'

'But you can't leave with a cloud over your head,' Annie protested. 'It will ruin your whole future, and it's such a bright future, Phil.'

'Is it?' he said, then, after touching Maggie lightly on the hand, he turned and left the room.

Maggie knew the rest of the team was looking at her, waiting for her to follow him—talk some sense into him—but her legs wouldn't have carried her anywhere and, as she felt her knees give way, she sank down onto the nearest chair.

Talk broke out around her, but she barely heard it, wondering what had pushed Phil to take this stance. Then she heard Alex calling for quiet.

'Are we all agreed we'll fight this business as a team and not let Phil accept the role of scapegoat?'

Loud noises of agreement.

'And that we'll fight whatever the hospital administrators want to throw at us?'

More agreement.

'Good,' Alex said. 'That's decided. Now, if you'll excuse me, I'll go find my fellow and beat some sense into his stupid head.'

He glanced Maggie's way but she shrugged away the unasked question. She was too confused herself to be able to offer any advice whatsoever.

'OK, let's get out of this place. How about the Thai

restaurant down the road? We can get that big table in the alcove and have some privacy to talk this through.'

Maggie was surprised to hear Kurt organising things, but Rachel, Ned, Scott and the theatre and nursing staff present all seemed content to follow his lead.

'I've work to finish here,' Annie said, 'but you lot go ahead.'

'I'll stay and help you,' Maggie told her, knowing she couldn't sit through a meal where Phil's position was being discussed.

'Do you know why he offered to resign?' Annie asked, when the others had departed.

'Because he's Phil!' Maggie said. 'There's a lot of old-fashioned gallantry, and ''doing the right thing'' in our Phil. He felt by sacrificing himself he'd save the unit.'

She sighed.

'He's been upset about that baby since it happened. Upset about all the babies that die. Maybe he's just had enough.'

But she knew it wasn't true. Losing a baby—a child—would only make Phil work harder to save the next one, make him learn more, try something different, test out the widest parameters—anything to save a child.

To save having one more baby crying in his head...

'He needs a break,' Annie said. 'Alex was saying as much the other day. Phil carried on when Alex was distracted by me being in hospital, then we had our honeymoon, but Phil hasn't had a holiday in over a year. The work's too emotionally fraught for them to just keep going.'

She was talking sense, but Maggie knew she was also waiting for a contribution from the woman who was supposedly engaged to Phil—herself. But she had nothing to contribute. She loved him, and knew more about him now than she had when they'd moved in together—knew things about him she doubted many people knew. But most of what went on in his head was a complete mystery.

There were no lights on at Maggie's place when she and Annie walked home an hour later.

'They must both be down at my place,' Annie said. 'Come home and have a bite to eat, and find out what's happening.'

Not wanting to go into the dark, empty house, Maggie agreed, although she doubted Phil would be at Annie's, a doubt confirmed when they walked in.

'He's taken leave, packed a bag and left for the airport. Reckons if he's standing there, a seat will turn up on a flight to London sooner or later.'

Alex explained this while he poured them each a glass of white wine.

You'll just have to forgive me this lapse, Maggie told the baby, taking the glass and sipping gratefully at the wine.

'Why London?' someone said, only realising who the someone was when Annie and Alex answered together.

'Because his family's there,' they chorused, and Maggie knew she couldn't tell them he didn't have a concept of 'family' in the way most people did.

But, still, they *were* his family, and maybe in times of stress everyone turned to family, no matter how dysfunctional they were.

He certainly hadn't turned to her!

Although he'd left her a note.

'Take care of yourself, Mags. I'll be back. Love, Phil.'

Love, Phil! Her brothers signed their emails with 'Love, Jonah' and 'Love, Ryan', even Tom occasionally added a 'love' to his sign-off 'T'. That kind of 'love' meant nothing.

'Not quite the kind of note you clutch to your heart and treasure for ever!' Maggie muttered, but she did fold it into four and tuck it into her pocket, patting it from time to time as she walked up the stairs to prepare for bed.

CHAPTER ELEVEN

SOMEHOW Maggie got through the next few days. Even before the court case drama blew up, Alex had asked Annie to juggle their operating load so he could give Phil some time off, so only simple operations were scheduled.

But having a less frenetic workload gave her more time to think, and she found herself missing Phil so badly she began to wonder if love had to be a two-way street for a marriage to work.

To make matters worse, the hospital's insurance company had appointed investigators, who were gathering information for a legal defence against the negligence claims. With Phil gone, they were targeting herself, Rachel and Kurt, making it obvious they were gunning for Alex's team and willing to throw the unit to the wolves in order to save the hospital's reputation.

'It's stupid,' Alex said, when he and Annie called in for a coffee after dinner. Knowing Maggie was lonely, they'd brought Minnie with them and suggested she stay with Maggie for a while. 'The hospital's defence team should be concentrating on the facts—on things like statistics showing the number of babies born with such defective hearts die anyway. On statistics showing the results of operations on neonates. They should be doing that, not badgering my staff about what happened during the op.'

'Their story is they have to know everything that happened because the other side could bring up something, and if they don't know about it, they can't argue against it.'

'Seems a strange way to be doing things,' Annie said, reaching out to pat Minnie who was snuggled up on Maggie's lap.

But Alex looked interested.

'Was there anything went on? Do you think there could have been a problem during the op?'

'The baby was on bypass for a long time. Kurt mentioned it at the time. And Rachel manually kept his heart beating just before he went on pump, but I've seen her do that when you and Phil were operating.'

Maggie paused and looked at Alex.

'I don't think we should be looking to blame our colleagues, even those from other hospitals,' she said quietly.

Alex nodded.

'You're right, but neither should we cover up mistakes. That's happened too often in the past in the world of medicine. The old joke that doctors can bury their mistakes has a lot of truth in it. Be fair, be honest in all you say, but try also to be detached. Tell it like it was without worrying about consequences. Think of the consequences of covering up a colleague's incompetence.'

Maggie nodded.

'I know what you're saying, and I've been totally honest about my recollections of the op. I've let them see my notes, but I can't and won't make judgements about the other staff's abilities or conduct. I know what I did and what Evan, who was the anaesthetist in charge, did, and I watched other stuff from time to time, and heard things like Kurt's comment, but I wouldn't have a clue if the surgeon tied the right kind of knot or not.'

Annie laughed, easing the tension that had grown in the room, but no amount of laughter could ease the tension that pervaded the unit over the next week.

'We can't go on like this for the rest of the year, or for however long it takes for the case to get to court,' Maggie said to Annie as they walked the two dogs in the park the following Saturday. 'Everyone's so uptight, something's got to give.'

'At least Pete and his father are both on the mend,' Maggie reminded her, although she too had wondered how long they could go on before something fired the tension into an explosion that would tear the whole unit apart.

'It would have been easier if the hospital administrators had stuck by us and tackled the case head on, rather than trying to weasel out of it by blaming us.'

'Why can't they blame Ellis?' Maggie asked. 'He's a consultant, not on staff.'

'Because he's the one that suggested the parents sue. I imagine they were so upset he used the suggestion to divert them. Probably didn't think they would, because he's not going to come out of this too well.'

'But it's Phil whose career will really suffer,' Maggie said, the sadness she carried within her pressing against her breastbone so she had to hold her hand against it for a moment.

'Yes,' Annie said, finishing the conversation, because there was nothing more to say.

Somewhere someone was making a terrible noise. At first Maggie thought it was in her dreams, but when she finally shook herself out of a deep sleep, she realised it was Minnie, barking furiously at the front door.

Clambering out of bed, Maggie grabbed her old chenille dressing-gown and wrapped it around her body. A quick glance at the clock told her it was well past midnight, and the fact that she could now hear knocking at the front door suggested it was unlikely to be a burglar asking to be let in.

Downstairs, she quietened Minnie by picking her up, then she turned on the porch light and peered through the spyhole. A bit of a blue and red striped tie, white shirt and suit lapels came into view, but try as she may she couldn't see a face.

'Who is it?' she called through the heavy door.

'Callan Park.'

She must be hearing things. Or the man wasn't very good at aliases. Even people from Melbourne knew the old mental asylum in Sydney had been called Callan Park. These days it housed a number of small organisations, but that didn't explain the man...

'Who?'

'Phil's brother, Callum. Callum Park.'

Oh!

'Phil's not here.'

That wasn't right, yelling such an unwelcoming statement through the door, but recent events had her dithering uncertainly.

'Phil's on his way,' the stranger said. 'We could only get one seat on the flight I came on, so he's following. He'll be here tomorrow morning but if you'd rather I went to a hotel, that's all right. But I've sent the cab away...'

Phil's on his way. The words rang like music in her ears and she opened the door.

'I'm sorry,' she said to Callum, who was frowning at her in exactly the way Phil so often did.

'No, I'm sorry,' he said, his beautiful voice making the words seem special. 'I should have phoned first, or asked Phil to phone. You really shouldn't be letting strangers into your house at any time, let alone at one in the morning.'

He looked so like Phil she smiled at him, and lifted Minnie higher for his inspection.

'Not even when I have my fierce watchdog to protect me?'

'Ah! This, I assume, is Minnie.'

He reached out to fondle the squirming dog.

'Why are you here? What's happening? Where's Phil been that he's flying in in the morning?'

'He's been home,' the man who looked like Phil said, then he leaned forward to kiss Maggie on the cheek. 'To see his family,' he added, then lifted his bag and looked expectantly at the steps. 'Spare bedroom upstairs?'

Totally bemused by now, Maggie nodded.

'Last door on the left,' she said. 'The bed's made up.'

'Great!' Callum announced, and he headed up the stairs. 'I can never sleep on planes, no matter how long they make the bed.'

Too awake—too excited—now to be able to consider sleeping, Maggie carried Minnie through to the kitchen, where she put the dog back in her basket, then opened the fridge, hoping to find something to munch on while she considered this latest development in her life.

Though it wasn't in *her* life, it was in Phil's.

His brother had come to visit—so what?

But no amount of plain talking to herself would banish the feeling of excitement simmering inside her.

Phil was coming back—that was part of it. But he was coming home as well, she felt sure of it.

Then the wetness came, and she knew exactly what was happening. She rested her head on the door of the fridge and cried.

Although her previous experiences of miscarriage had been so long ago, she still remembered how it would progress. She couldn't stay leaning on the fridge for much longer.

On leaden legs she made her way up to her bathroom, turned on the shower, stripped off her clothes and stood under the cascading water while her hopes and dreams, and an embryo barely three centimetres long, were washed away.

Her tears mingled with the cleansing water—tears for the baby, for Phil and what might, in time, have been. Then she began to shiver—the water was running cold. She left the refuge of the shower stall, dried herself, pulled on a comfortable old flannel nightdress and crawled into bed.

Later today—no, today was Sunday, tomorrow—she'd see a doctor, book in for a curette, do what had to be done and maybe even arrange for tests to find out why she couldn't carry a baby.

Though she doubted she'd worry about the tests...

She doubted it would ever be important.

Her heart felt as if the blood was seeping out of it—her life washing away with that of the tiny embryo.

She woke to find the day had begun without her, bright sunshine streaming through her window.

Too bright, too sunshiny! It should have been raining—gloomy as her mood. Dull as the ache in her chest.

She pulled on her dressing-gown and headed downstairs. At least she could drink real coffee now. Cups and cups of it.

And focus on her career again—on saving the lives of other babies.

She was at the bottom of the stairs before she heard the voices and remembered she had a visitor. But voices? Was he talking to himself?

Minnie! He'd be talking to Minnie.

But such common-sense explanations didn't cut it with her body, which was showing all the signs it usually did when Phil was in the vicinity.

Phil—what would Phil think?

He'd be relieved.

He'd have to be.

The thought made her even sadder and she swallowed hard.

No self-pity!

Neither would she dash back upstairs—to hide or even to change into something more attractive.

Maggie continued doggedly on her way.

Phil was sitting in his usual chair, Minnie on his lap, his brother opposite him, and, most surprising of all, Annie and Alex were also at the table.

But it was Phil who saw her first, his face breaking into a smile that faded as she watched. Then he was on his feet, depositing Minnie on the floor, walking towards Maggie and taking her arm, guiding her out of the kitchen, out of earshot and away from watching eyes, then taking her in his arms and holding her close for a long, long minute.

He cuddled her close, murmured her name then kissed her on the top of her head, before easing away so he could look at her.

'Mags! What is it? Are you OK? Is it the baby?'

Maggie couldn't answer. Oh, there were heaps of things she'd have liked to say. *Why should anything be wrong?* would be a starter, and *Why should you care about the baby?* should follow straight after it. But her voice wouldn't work and Phil must have realised it for he folded her once again into his arms and whispered, 'Oh, love,' in such a broken voice it was all she could do not to burst into tears all over again.

'When did it happen?' he asked, still holding her tightly.

'Last night.'

'Damn that Ellis. I should have been here. Mags, I'm sorrier than I can ever say! Sorry I wasn't here, but sorry too about the baby.' His voice cracked as he added, 'Our baby!'

Maggie let him hold her, drawing strength from his arms and warmth from the genuine sense of loss she could hear in his voice. Then his arms tightened and he was talking again, saying things she'd never thought to hear—saying things she hardly dared believe.

'But there'll be other babies, Mags. For both of us— and if there aren't then we'll still have each other.'

He tilted up her chin and kissed her on the lips.

'We will have each other, won't we?' he whispered, his usually confident voice shaky with emotion. 'Because I love you, Maggie Walsh, with all my heart and mind and soul. You asked me for my love once and I backed away, offered no guarantee, but that was before I realised how important you are to me—far more important than a fantasy cottage with fantasy roses climbing over the door. More important, Mags, than life it-self.'

He held her for a long time, rocking her back and forth, then he lifted her into his arms, carried her up the stairs and tucked her back into bed, taking control both of his emotions and the situation—being practical—talking all the time.

'Stay there. You're sheet-white. You don't look after yourself properly. I'll get you something. Coffee and toast? I'll send the lot in the kitchen down to Annie's house to talk and we'll have this place to ourselves. Stay right there. Don't move. I'll be right back.'

Maggie stared at him, still trying to make sense of what was happening.

All of what was happening…

'You love me?' she whispered, and won a funny, twisted kind of smile from Phil.

'So much you wouldn't believe,' he told her, the half-smile still hovering around his lips. 'But food first. I'm famished, too. I don't know how that can be because I did nothing but eat on the plane.'

He bent and kissed her—hard—then left the room.

Maggie stared up at the ceiling, wondering how one person could be so sad yet so happy at the same time. And she was really perfectly OK—physically—so why had she submitted to Phil's fussing?

Especially when a meeting of some importance was obviously going on downstairs.

But Phil was here—he'd said he loved her and now he was bringing coffee and toast, so she snuggled down deeper into the bed and waited for him to come back.

'Callum's a barrister who did medicine first then switched to law so he's become an expert in medico-legal work,' Phil explained, much later, when he was lying back against the pillows on the other side of her bed.

They'd talked about her miscarriage, established she'd do all the right things as far as seeing doctors went and held each other close again to ease the ache of loss. Then practicality had exerted itself and they'd demolished a large plate of toast and strawberry jam. Now Maggie was savouring her first real coffee in ages and watching the man she loved as he sought for the words he wanted to say to her.

'You made me think of Cal,' Phil added, turning so he could kiss Maggie's cheek. 'You and your talk of home and family. He'd been in my mind for a while— he and Laura, my sister. So when this blew up, I thought I'd go and see him, to talk about the case but also to talk about other things. About our upbringing and family and what it meant to him and Laura. The problem was, we hadn't ever talked about it. We'd been close as children—united against the world when we were small—but then we all went off to boarding school and saw so little of each other that the sibling closeness seemed to fade away.'

Maggie put her coffee cup on the bedside table and moved so she could hold his hand, her body pressed closer to his, although she was in the bed and he was on it.

Phil kissed her cheek again, as if in thanks, then lifted her hand to his lips and kissed the back of it.

'I let it fade away, Mags,' he said. 'I told myself it didn't matter. Oh, I always saw Cal and Laura when I was in the UK—we'd have a drink, a meal, but that was it. We never talked.'

Maggie turned to look at him and saw the tiredness of travel in his face, but below that there was warmth, as if he'd found something special that had been missing from his life for a long time.

'You talked this time?' she prompted quietly.

Phil beamed at her.

'Talked and talked, all three of us. We even dragged Mother in at the end and talked with her as well.'

He hesitated and then added, 'I found I had a family after all.'

Maggie swallowed the lump in her throat—couldn't blame hormones this time—and tried to concentrate on where this conversation had begun.

'And Callum?' she asked, but Phil was sound asleep, a small smile of contentment lingering on his face.

Maggie rolled over so she was curled against his body, though a sheet, two blankets and an eiderdown separated them, and went quietly off to sleep herself.

Callum stayed a fortnight, spending most of his time locked in conference with hospital officials and insurance officers, making it exceedingly clear the unit staff would not accept anything less than complete exoneration in the tragic death of the baby.

'You've got to see something of Australia while you're here,' Phil told him, late in his visit, on one of the rare occasions he, Maggie and Cal were eating dinner together at home. 'You can't go back to England without seeing anything of the country.'

'Not this time,' Cal said. 'But I'll take a month's leave when I come out for your and Maggie's wedding, and do some travelling then.'

'Wedding?' Maggie said.

Cal smiled at her.

'Don't tell me he hasn't asked you yet! He was like that as a small boy—always putting things off because he felt there had to be a perfect moment to do or ask whatever it was. Of course, there's never a perfect moment.'

'I think there are,' Maggie said stoutly, thinking of the whispered 'Oh, love' she still carried in her heart.

'Don't tell him that,' Cal groaned. 'You'll never get him up to the mark.'

'Have you ever thought Maggie might not want me?' Phil said.

'Drivel! Of course she wants you. Even Minnie knows she's head over heels in love with you.'

The little dog, hearing her name, came to sit at Callum's feet.

'Don't you, Min?' he added, and Maggie was grateful his attention had been diverted as she knew her cheeks would be scarlet with embarrassment.

Phil did know she loved him—she'd told him so—but she wasn't going to let his brother bully him into doing something he didn't want to do.

'Love's just a word that has different meanings in different contexts,' she told Callum. 'Some love is transient, ephemeral—not strong enough to build a relationship on, let alone a marriage. Marriage is about for ever and the love you need for that is gut-deep.'

Then, embarrassed by the conversation, she stood up.

'I've got to go back up to the hospital for a while,' she said, knowing Phil would insist on walking up with her. 'When you boys finish arguing you can stack the dishwasher.'

Phil was on his feet before she reached the door.

'You can't walk up there in the dark on your own. Callum can stack. I'll come with you.'

Maggie smiled to herself, partly because she'd been

right in her prediction but also because there'd been so much going on, and with Callum in the house she and Phil had spent very little time together.

'I'm OK,' she said to him, when they were walking out the gate. 'I understand where things stand between us. Even if you do love me, we want such different things from marriage it would never work, so don't let your brother bully you into doing something you don't want to do.'

She was holding his hand because it seemed a natural thing to do, and she felt his response in the pressure of his fingers.

'It's hard, Mags,' he said, drawing her closer, their hands still clasped together. 'Hard because what Callum said is true—I do put off important things, thinking there should be an optimum moment. And what you said is true about knowing where things stand—or it was true, up until the time I went away. That's when I realised how much you meant to me. Far more than any dream of a picture-perfect home, or some image of a stay-at-home wife. I went to see Callum as a barrister who would help us with the court case and ended up seeing him as a brother, because suddenly it was important to me that I had a family— that I understood family as you understand it.'

He stopped and turned towards her.

'It was important for me to learn what family meant, because I knew I didn't have a hope of persuading you to marry me if I was still vague about the concept. And if I didn't understand it, then I'd lose my wise, passionate and, oh, so compassionate Maggie.'

He paused and brushed a kiss across her lips.

'I had to learn that home and family are about people, not places—that it's the people and the love they share that makes a family complete, that makes any place they dwell in home. For some reason I'd let my fantasy tarnish the love I feel for my own family, and let it blind me to the love the members of it have for me.'

He paused again, to kiss her once more, but also to draw breath because he hadn't finished all he had to say.

'But I know the difference now, Mags, between fantasy and reality. You're reality—you and me. That's reality. But I needed to leave you—to be away from you—to realise just how much I love you. Love you gut-deep—I couldn't have put it any better.'

She looked up into his face, and saw the plea in the way he stood, and read anxiety in his eyes.

They were near the main road now, the footpath too brightly lit for them to see the stars. The air was redolent with petrol and diesel fumes, and the only music was the roar of traffic, the occasional squeal of brakes and the occasional blare of a car horn.

'Is this the perfect moment you've been looking for?' Maggie teased, and Phil let out a huge sigh of relief, gathered her in his arms and kissed her soundly.

'Woohoo!' a young voice cried, and two teenagers skirted around them.

'I love you, Mags. Will you marry me?' Phil asked, and Maggie snuggled close to him again and nodded.

'No, I need to hear the words,' he said, so Maggie looked up at him and said just one word.

'Yes.'

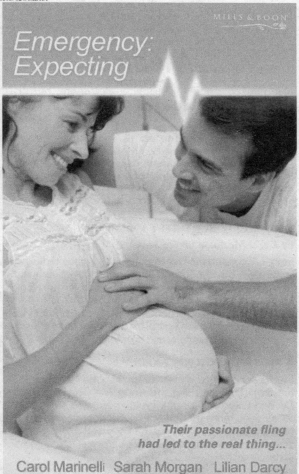

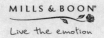

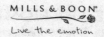

MILLS & BOON

THE
WEDDING
CHASE

Three eligible young rakes were about to be caught...

KASEY MICHAELS
GAYLE WILSON
LYN STONE

On sale 1st July 2005

Available at most branches of WHSmith, Tesco, ASDA, Martins, Borders, Eason, Sainsbury's and all good paperback bookshops.

FREE!

4 Books
and a surprise gift!

We would like to take this opportunity to thank you for reading this Mills & Boon® book by offering you the chance to take FOUR more specially selected titles from the Medical Romance™ series absolutely FREE! We're also making this offer to introduce you to the benefits of the Reader Service™—

- ★ **FREE home delivery**
- ★ **FREE gifts and competitions**
- ★ **FREE monthly Newsletter**
- ★ **Exclusive Reader Service offers**
- ★ **Books available before they're in the shops**

Accepting these FREE books and gift places you under no obligation to buy, you may cancel at any time, even after receiving your free shipment. Simply complete your details below and return the entire page to the address below. You don't even need a stamp!

YES! Please send me 4 free Medical Romance books and a surprise gift. I understand that unless you hear from me, I will receive 6 superb new titles every month for just £2.75 each, postage and packing free. I am under no obligation to purchase any books and may cancel my subscription at any time. The free books and gift will be mine to keep in any case.

M5ZEE

Ms/Mrs/Miss/Mr ....Initials...
BLOCK CAPITALS PLEASE

Surname ....

Address..

....

....Postcode ....

Send this whole page to:
UK: FREEPOST CN81, Croydon, CR9 3WZ